Dear Romance Reader,

Welcome to a world of breathtaking passion and never-ending romance.

Welcome to *Precious Gem Romances*.

It is our pleasure to present *Precious Gem Romances*, a wonderful new line of romance books by some of America's best-loved authors. Let these thrilling historical and contemporary romances sweep you away to far-off times and places in stories that will dazzle your senses and melt your heart.

Sparkling with joy, laughter, and love, each *Precious Gem Romance* glows with all the passion and excitement you expect from the very best in romance. Offered at a great affordable price, these books are an irresistible value—and an essential addition to your romance collection. Tender love stories you will want to read again and again, *Precious Gem Romances* are books you will treasure forever.

Look for fabulous new *Precious Gem Romances* each month—available only at Wal★Mart.

Kate Duffy
Editorial Director

# MUST
# BE
# MAGIC

## CHARLENE SUMMERS

Zebra Books
Kensington Publishing Corp.
http://www.zebrabooks.com

ZEBRA BOOKS are published by

Kensington Publishing Corp.
850 Third Avenue
New York, NY 10022

First Printing: June, 1999
10 9 8 7 6 5 4 3 2 1

Printed in the United States of America

To Don, the boy with the soft blue eyes who grew up to be the man of my dreams, my husband and best friend. I treasure the constant and unyielding faith you have in me. You are always the heart of my inspiration.

# ONE

Faith McAllister slipped into the emerald-green dress and stared at her reflection in the mirror. "I don't know, Hope. This dress is too suggestive. Maybe I should change." With both hands she tugged at the hem, but the clingy material had memory and simply went right back into place.

Faith's sister sidled up next to her and their eyes met. "Don't be silly, sis, you look great. The dark green matches your eyes. It's perfect for my wedding rehearsal."

Perfect, yes—but not necessarily for a wedding. The dress had served its purpose well one year ago, when Faith had one thing on her mind—seduction. Those memories had been tucked safely away, until Hope dragged the dress out of the far corner of the closet, insisting she wear it tonight. Faith had forgotten she still owned the dress, having worn it only that one fateful night.

But to wear the slinky dress to Hope's wedding rehearsal, then dinner afterward? She continued to scrutinize herself in the mirror, tilting her head to get a different perspective. She tried lifting the material over her exposed cleavage. When she released the fabric, it snapped down even lower on her chest. She groaned. "I can't."

"Yessss, you can!" Hope responded with her usual flair for the dramatic. "And quit tugging, you're going to stretch it all out of shape."

"Hope, it's just not me."

Hope whispered in her ear, "It's you, sister dear, you just haven't realized it yet. And in that get-up, you'll attract every available male in the vicinity. It can't hurt to get back into circulation. Remember, there will be lots of single men at my wedding tomorrow. Some of Tony's real estate agents are really cute."

Faith shrugged and gave up adjusting the dress. "At twenty-eight years old, I'm beyond wanting 'cute.' Besides, I have Bill."

Hope's lips turned down as they often did when Faith mentioned Bill's name. "You mean, Old William."

Faith rolled her eyes heavenward. Her sister did not approve of Faith dating an older man. Faith liked Bill as a friend and together they shared a love of books and fine arts. "I enjoy his company."

"Oh, Faith, what you need is passion, excitement. You're stagnating." Hope lowered her voice and said emphatically, "I'd love to see you spice up your life, preferably with some studly guy who knows how to treat a woman."

Faith had tried that once. She had no one to blame but herself. Hurt and confused after her fiancé, Peter, had dumped her, Faith sought the ultimate revenge. And to this day, she hadn't forgiven herself.

What she'd done wasn't a crime, she told herself over and over. But Faith had a conscience that wouldn't allow rationalizing. She should have been arrested for the wanton way she had behaved—in the name of what? Revenge? Defiance? Anger?

But she'd never forget the way she'd felt that night in the arms of that stranger. Tall, dark, brooding. Mysterious. She'd known very little about him but his name. She'd insisted on that.

Nick.

He'd been relentless.

And he had made love to her as if she were the only woman on the planet he cared about, the only woman he wanted. At that point in her life, Faith needed those reassurances. Her heart had been broken and her ego badly bruised. Faith sighed.

"Since Bill won't be in town for the wedding, you can hang out with the best man. Chandler is Tony's best friend and he's gorgeous." Hope picked up a silver-plated brush from the vanity and began brushing Faith's long auburn hair.

Faith ignored the matchmaking gleam in her sister's eyes. "I thought you've never met him."

"Once, quite some time ago. But I think he'll be in town for a while. He's got a project here. You know the type, a man of few words, but loads of body language." Hope's face lit up. "It wouldn't hurt for you two to become . . . friendly."

"Hope." Faith put a warning tone in her voice. Her sister had a knack for scheming when it came to Faith's love life.

"Tony adores him," Hope rushed out. "They grew up together. He's had some bad breaks in life. Tony says he's a real good guy, though. I like him. I think you will too."

"Don't start, okay? I'm not shopping for romance." Faith snatched the hairbrush out of her sister's hands and turned to face her. "Bill will do just fine."

Faith had learned her lesson last year in the arms of a stranger. She wasn't as flamboyant and confident as her sister. The one time she'd tried to break out of the shell Hope kept alluding to, Faith had failed miserably. And she hadn't told another soul about her hot one-night fling, not even the sister she loved with all of her heart.

Sharing a condominium with Hope was her only real taste of excitement. Suddenly, Faith realized how much she was going to miss her sister when she moved out. The two of them had lived together for the last five years.

Faith threw her arms around her sister. "Oh Hope, nothing will be the same around here after you're gone."

Hope clung to her. "You mean you'll actually miss my teasing and pestering?"

"Of course, I've never minded. Except, maybe, your meddling with my personal life."

Hope planted a quick kiss on her cheek. "I think you'll miss that too. But honey, you know Tony and I will only be a few minutes away. And we want you around. You won't be intruding."

"You'll want to toss me out on my butt, you'll get so sick of seeing me." She winked to hide the heartfelt emotion bubbling inside of her. Her sister would be sorely missed. "But enough of this mushy stuff. Let's hurry. Your prince charming will be picking you up soon. The wedding rehearsal starts in just one hour."

* * *

Saint Charles Catholic Church looked like a small cathedral, built with high arches and beautifully sculpted walls that were complemented by tall stained glass windows. Faith loved this old church. It reminded her so much of her parish in Chicago, where she'd spent many a Sunday morning sitting in the pews as a young girl, imagining her wedding day.

She stood in the vestibule, absently gazing at a marble statue, knowing for certain her sister's marriage wouldn't be plagued by the Triple Charm—a string of misfortune that seemed to have besieged the females in her family for close to one hundred years. To call it a marriage curse while anointing herself with holy water would seem sacrilegious. But in truth, throughout recent history, the women on her mother's side of the family had been notorious for their bad choices in men. It had taken her mother three times to finally get it right by marrying Frank McAllister. Rachel O'Leary's first marriage had been annulled after three weeks, and she'd been engaged for seven years preceding that before breaking it off with the fellow. Then, at the ripe old age of thirty-five, her mother had met Frank and settled down.

The same held true for Faith's grandmother and her grandmother's mother before that. For as long as anyone could remember, it took three good solid tries before the females of the clan truly met their soul mate. They called it the Triple Charm. To signify its importance, three gold charms in the shape of clover leaves were worn on a delicate bracelet by the oldest unmarried female member of the family.

Faith was certain her sister Hope's marriage to Tony DiMartino was based on solid ground. Hope had broken off two previous engagements, which made Tony number three. Their marriage was sure to survive and Faith was thrilled Tony would be the one. In the span of the year's time, she'd already come to think of him as a brother. The curse or charm, whichever way one chose to look upon it, hadn't been broken in more than ninety years.

As crazy as it seemed, rational, level-headed Faith McAllister believed in the Triple Charm with all her heart. Some things were beyond question, beyond reason.

Faith tugged at the hem of her skimpy dress to no avail, berating herself for giving in to her sister about wearing it. Guiltily, she looked up at the stained glass saints peering down at her from the tall, arched windows, and groaned. With haste, she entered into the back of the church and hoped the rehearsal wouldn't take too long.

Hope, beaming with joy, came rushing down the aisle. "There you are. We're just about to get started." She snagged Faith's arm, urging her to the front of the church. "I'd hoped to introduce you to the best man, but he's been detained. We're going to start without him."

Faith knew everyone else. Two of Hope's good friends greeted her, as did Tony's older brothers, and the bridesmaids and ushers. Father Ryan, the friendly, ruddy-faced priest who had baptized Tony and his brothers, would preside over the ceremony.

"You'd think he'd show up on time for Tony's wedding rehearsal," Faith whispered in her sister's ear when the others had been assigned their positions.

"Tony said he'd be here. He trusts him."

Faith had little trust in most men, especially after what her former fiancé had done to her. She stifled an unladylike snort and again glanced up at the saints. They seemed to be glaring down at her this time. Faith told herself to quit imagining things. With that accomplished, she plastered on a broad smile, took her place in line in front of Hope, and listened for her cue to begin the walk down the long carpeted aisle.

"Just think how the church will look tomorrow with ribbons, bows, and flowers everywhere," Hope said with a wistful sigh.

Faith turned to look at her sister. Hope's eyes were glowing with a beautiful green-blue sparkle that warmed the chilly anteroom. Faith had never seen her sister so happy. "I think you'll steal the show. You'll be the most beautiful bride to ever walk down this aisle."

Hope chuckled softly. "Thank you. I think I needed that. I'm so . . . jittery."

"Excited, from the look on your face."

"Yes, I love Tony with all my heart. I can't believe it's happening, Faith. I'm finally getting the man of my dreams."

"I'm happy for you, Hope."

Hope smiled then, looking down at the charm bracelet adorning her wrist. She unlatched the fine gold chain, lifted up Faith's hand and dropped the bracelet into her palm. With ceremony, she closed her fingers around Faith's hand and drew in a deep breath. "It's your turn for happiness. Wear this well."

Faith swallowed hard and looked at her closed hand, feeling the dainty antique bracelet tickle her palm, knowing the significance of wearing the charm. Tears stung her eyes. All of her female ancestors had worn this charm bracelet, all they way back to their Irish roots in Dublin more than ninety years ago. This was their legacy. What had started out as a source of amusement had held firm through the years, and the charm with all its mystical powers had survived through to the present time.

Faith glanced down and fingered each charm. If the magic held true for her, then Peter had been number one. She'd been jilted and had come to terms with the fact. It meant one more heartbreak was in store for her before she could find true love. Could she endure the pain again, the humiliation? Why must all the women in her family face such agony?

But she knew the answer. And it was written all over her sister's glowing face. What Hope had found in Tony could never be rivaled.

Grandmother Betsy had once said that she still tingled from head to toe when Grandpa Edward walked through the door at night. Faith had been too young to understand then, but those words and the love in her grandparents' eyes when they looked at each other now made complete sense. At the ripe old age of seventy-nine, the two had remained lovebirds, doting on each other with adoration.

Faith fastened the bracelet onto her wrist and dangled her hand. Confident it was secure, she wrapped her arms around her sister. "I feel so . . ."

"Overwhelming, isn't it?" Hope asked, once they had broken their quick embrace. "Just remember. Don't tell anyone why you wear it, especially a man you might . . . well, just don't trust any man with the truth, until you're sure he's the one."

"I've never understood why that is."

"I was told the charm will lose its magic."

"And you believe that?"

"Faith." Her sister glanced around. "It's like Dad used to say about Santa Claus and the Tooth Fairy—if you choose not to believe, they are sure not to come."

"But that's different."

"Shhh. Listen, that's your cue. Father Ryan just called for the maid of honor." Hope chuckled, giving Faith a little shove. "Start walking, we're keeping my husband-to-be waiting."

Faith stood facing the long aisle and when Father Ryan motioned, she began her trek. She glanced at Tony's smiling face and returned his smile. Just then, a quick movement by the bridegroom's side caught her attention. A man hastily made his entrance from the side doors and took his position next to Tony. So, the wayward best man finally decided to show up. Chandler. She watched Tony turn to shake his hand, then pat him on the back. And then both sets of eyes turned her way.

Tony's gaze still held merriment, but as Faith glanced to the best man, he honed in on her like a hawk. His eyes changed instantly from openly friendly to narrowed, dark, and definitely not friendly.

A blast of cold raced through her, chilling her bones. She thought she knew this man but that wasn't possible, was it? Convinced her eyes were deceiving her, she forced herself to continue.

Faith's smile wavered, but she managed to put one shaky foot in front of the other as she made her way down the aisle. She dared another glance at Tony's best man. His stark, cold appraisal made her knees go weak. And the closer she got, the more she realized she was not mistaken. She'd never forget those intense, mysterious eyes. It *was* him!

Oh no! Frantic, Faith chewed her lip. Panic clenched her gut. She had nowhere to run, nowhere to hide; she had to continue her walk down the aisle. But her head spun in circles and the church seemed to be brilliantly illuminated all of a sudden. All around her, light poured in. Yes, the light surrounded her now, all over. The dizzying glow released her fear. Her legs went weak. She felt herself sway, then drop onto the floor. A sharp thump at the base of her head brought her quickly back to reality faster than any smelling salts might. Dazed, she tried to sit up. She heard voices.

"Oh dear! She's fainted! Don't move, Faith."

"She's hit her head on the pew, poor thing."

"Somebody, get some ice!"

Unfortunately, *he* was the first one to reach her. Dark-haired, dusky-eyed and more devilishly handsome than she remembered, his sharp gaze held her attention. Strong, powerful hands encased hers, bringing back a memory of another time. "Are you hurt?"

The rich, painfully sexy voice made her shudder. "N-no, y-yes, my head." She lifted her head again slightly. "Nick?"

The white light returned, brighter than before. Her eyes fell closed. She heard a low whisper in the distance before the brilliant lights in her head snapped off.

"She's fainted again."


Nick Chandler sat in the last pew of the church with his head in his hands. A whirlwind of emotions played havoc with his stomach and as it clenched involuntarily, he stifled a curse, reminding himself where he was.

He'd spent many a Sunday at mass with Tony and his family. And had been reprimanded time and again for ducking out before the psalms were over. Mary DiMartino had been an angel for putting up with him. Tony's mother had taken him in, and no matter how much trouble he'd caused, the boy from the wrong side of the tracks always had a place to call home.

Maybe this was his retribution for all the gum-chewing, the ripped missal pages and the wiser-than-thou attitude of his youth. Seeing *her* again, after all this time. He had often daydreamed about bumping into the redhead, then casually walking away as if nothing had happened between them.

Heather O'Leary, she'd called herself. Hah! She'd lied to him, played him for a fool, run out on him. And now he learned that Faith McAllister was her real name, and that she was going to be Tony's sister-in-law.

Faith, of all names.

He'd been stunned for one brief moment, seeing her. Having Tony proudly point out his new *sister*. But that surprise hadn't lasted. No. Nick Chandler and bad luck were close companions. Nothing really shocked him anymore. He was a walking testimony to hard luck and bad timing. Today, he'd received a healthy dose of both.

Oh, but seeing her again, for one brief second, brought back images of a lovely pliant woman in his arms. A woman who for one glorious night had made him feel whole again.

Then anger, or rather rage, set in. He'd been glad to see her unease in that one fabulous moment when she'd recognized him. But then she had fainted, hitting her head so solidly, and fear for her safety had sent him rushing past everyone in the church to see to her.

Stupid.

He glanced up to view her, sitting upright in the first pew, with swarms of people attending her. The back of her head was resting on a folded towel. She'd probably have a nice lump there. Serves her right, he thought, then bounded up from the bench. He had to get out of here.

"Hey, Chandler," Tony called out, "looks like my new sister is going to be all right. She insists we all go to dinner. Come on up here and meet her officially."

Nick drew in a deep breath. Damn. Tony was the best friend he'd ever had. He was more like family than a friend. Nick wouldn't do anything to spoil his wedding, so he took the steps necessary to bring him square in front of Faith.

Tony tapped him on the shoulder. "Nick Chandler, this is going to be my new baby sister, Faith Heather McAllister. And Faith, you can thank Nick here for reaching you first. He carried you to the bench."

Faith stared at Nick's shoulder, probably afraid to look him in the eye, but as soon as Tony's introduction was over, she did look at him. Her incredible green eyes met his, and Nick felt an unmistakable tightening in his gut. He put out his hand and cautioned her with a look. "Nice to meet you, Faith."

Faith squirmed a little, then took his hand. She silently thanked him with her eyes for not revealing their secret. "It's nice to finally meet you, too. And thanks for coming to my . . . rescue."

Nick shrugged. "Sure, rescuing damsels is my specialty," he said, giving Faith a look meant only for her.

She blinked, then rubbed the back of her head.

"Nasty fall you took." He couldn't help tormenting her a little. "You looked as if you'd seen a ghost or something."

"It's all this excitement," Tony interrupted. "Faith's not used to so much commotion, right, Faith? The library's more your speed, although Hope and I encourage you to get out more," Tony expounded.

"The library?" Nick asked, trying to keep the amusement out of his tone. She'd told him an entirely different story. This one, he was dying to hear.

"Yes, she runs the Woodland Hills library."

Nick glanced at Faith. So his hot-blooded one-nighter was the town librarian, not the glamorous interior designer she'd pretended to be. Her lips quivered and although most of the color had come back to her face, he found her turning the color of curdled milk now.

"A librarian, how commendable," Nick said dryly.

"She's got a master's degree. Faith knows more about books than anyone I know." Tony spoke with pride. He obviously thought well of his future sister-in-law.

"That's because your head's only in the multiple listings," put in Louie, Tony's oldest brother. Everyone chuckled, even Tony.

Hope brushed past the crowd to face her sister.

"It's all set at the restaurant. Faith, are you sure about this?"

Faith winced when she nodded. Concern brought the corners of Hope's mouth down. "I won't be the one to hold up your dinner, Hope. I'm fine. Truly. Let's go eat."

But her words were far more enthusiastic than her movements. She got up from the bench gingerly with Hope holding one arm and Tony taking the other. "Maybe we should take you to the emergency room instead."

"No, please, Hope. I'm fine."

"You've never fainted before."

"And I won't again. I promise. You can both let go of me. I am just fine." Faith hoisted her chin defiantly.

The worried couple released her slowly. "Okay, but Nick here could give you a lift to the restaurant," Hope suggested.

"No! I mean—I don't want to burden anyone."

Hope looked at her sister, then eyed Nick. "She shouldn't be driving. I'm sure you wouldn't mind, would you, Nick?"

What could he say? He was boxed into a corner. "I'd be glad to."

Panicked, Faith touched his arm. Nick winced inwardly. Her touch still had impact, even though he wanted nothing further to do with her. "You don't have to. Really. I'll ride with my sister."

"Uh, honey, Tony picked me up in the Porsche, remember."

Faith looked helpless, biting her lip, searching for someone else to offer her a ride. No one did. Nick took hold of her elbow. "She'll ride with me. I'll get her there safe and sound."

Tony thanked him with an appreciative nod and ushered a worried Hope out of the church. The others followed behind.

Standing beside her, Nick made the mistake of looking down. She wore the same dress he'd met her in, the emerald-green number that flattered her incredible eyes and clung to her curves like a second skin. From his point of view, two beautifully sculpted breasts, barely contained in the soft fabric, tempted him. He'd given in to that temptation, once, and it had been memorable.

Suddenly, the red-hot night of passion they'd shared flashed through his memory, and the most poignant, intimate moments returned with vivid clarity. Her body under his, wet and wild as she cried out his name, her long satiny legs tangled in the sheets with his. Nick abruptly released her elbow.

*Not again, Nick. Not with this woman. She played you for a sucker. Forget the way she felt all soft and cuddly in your arms and remember how she ran out on you.*

"You coming, Irish?" he asked, striding ahead, no longer caring whether she was or not.

Her softly spoken words echoed in the empty church. "I'm coming, Nick."

Nick stumbled on the steps, remembering all too well, the last time the seductive redhead uttered those very words to him.

# TWO

Faith seated herself primly in the passenger seat. Nick slammed the door and strode around to his side of the car. She focused on him as he eased himself into the driver's seat. His motions were smooth and graceful, like those of an elegant steed. But Faith knew he was more dangerous than an entire herd of wild horses. Whatever had possessed her one year ago to link up with this man, however briefly, certainly wasn't compelling her at the moment.

She subdued the cold shiver threatening to race down her spine, and adjusted the hem of her dress. The clingy material climbed further up her leg. Nick didn't miss her attempt. With an arch of his brow, he stated matter-of-factly, "That dress would tempt a saint."

"I don't see any saints around here." Faith mustered a defiant tone.

He took his eyes off the road to glare at her. "Neither do I."

Properly put in her place, Faith clamped her mouth shut and stared at the scenery as they made their way through the high cliffs of Malibu Canyon to the Pacific seashore.

Blue-green water splashed upon the sun-caressed

sand and lathered the shore with lacy foam as she gazed at the ocean to her left. Purple wildflowers dotted intermittently with green foliage ran alongside the mountain that rose to her right. At any other time, Faith would appreciate the view for all its splendor as an orange-gold sun began its slow descent on the horizon, but now, she could only aim her gaze straight ahead and try to be calm.

As Nick drove with subdued hostility, Faith put her hand to her head. It wasn't the bump above her nape that gave her trouble, but rather the pensive, quiet man sitting beside her. In the silence, Faith's gaze wandered to his hand adjusting the gearshift, and the way the muscles in his thigh bunched when he applied the brakes.

The throbbing in her head continued. Memories of those hands on her trembling body and those powerful thighs meshing with hers made her stir uncomfortably. Nick's deep voice broke the silence. "Head hurting?"

"Not really." She fingered the back of her head, feeling the small bump. "I'm okay."

Nick pulled over his black Acura to the mountain side of the road and made an abrupt stop. "Well, I'm not."

Faith's mouth dropped open, but words wouldn't come. She wet her lips and caught Nick's sharp gaze perusing her mouth. He lifted dark, solemn eyes to her. "No small talk, Faith," he sneered. "I want some answers."

Faith crossed her arms over her middle. The material of her dress stretched down, exposing even more cleavage. She groaned silently. Nick Chandler would never believe she wasn't the seductive, inviting woman he'd met in Palm Springs. That woman had been bold, brazen, flirtatious. Faith had *invented* Heather O'Leary and played the role of a slinky, stylish woman of the nineties. Faith McAllister, librarian, really wasn't that sort of woman. And she wouldn't ever be.

She kept her gaze directed straight ahead. Inside, her stomach recoiled. "I see no need to rehash—"

Nick took hold of her wrist and said with determination, "I do."

Faith closed her eyes. Okay, maybe the man deserved some answers. "I never thought I'd see you again." She turned in the seat to face him. He sat with a hand resting on the steering wheel and his body turned in her direction.

He snorted and released her wrist. "That's obvious. Must have been quite a shock."

Frowning, Faith replied, "It was."

"Are you in the habit—"

"No!" Suddenly, she cared whether or not he believed she wasn't a woman of loose morals. She didn't know if she could make him understand. He slumped back in his seat and stared at her. "I don't usually . . . I mean I'd never before . . ." Faith drew in a deep breath, trying to produce the words that would appease his curiosity and justify what she'd done.

Nick ran a hand through his hair and shook his head. "You ran out on—you ran out in a hurry the next day."

Faith felt miserable. She'd put that night behind her, although it had taken her months. And now, here was this man dredging it all up. Heavens, how could he know how mortified she'd been the next day, thinking about the way she'd practically attacked him. Seduced might be a more accurate term. But in Faith's mind, she hadn't given the man a choice.

Nonsense, her rational side argued. Nick hadn't exactly been innocent himself, what with his practiced lines and smooth talk. His dark beckoning eyes alone were enough to make just about any sane female go weak in the knees.

"I doubt you're going to believe me, but the truth is . . . I was shocked at the way I'd behaved."

Nick's gaze flowed over her entire body from head to toe. It was as though he'd touched her intimately. And he took his sweet time answering. "You're right, I don't believe you."

Faith shrugged. "Then this discussion is pointless."

"I need a reason."

Faith balked at his tone and his demand. She hadn't been the only one in the hotel room that night. "Maybe I do too."

His eyes narrowed, but his lips curved up in a grin so sensual, Faith was robbed of breath. "You want my reason? I was feeling low, had a bummer of a day, then this hot, sexy woman enters the bar and every male head turns. The woman chooses me. Now, I'm feeling pretty lucky when she throws herself at me." He cocked his head to one side. "It wasn't in me to resist."

Blood rushed up Faith's neck and the heat of humiliation burned her cheeks. She'd asked for his reason, but she hadn't expected such a blunt and brutal assessment. The malicious gleam in his eyes had her lifting the door handle of the car. Within seconds, she was out, slamming the door and heading up the emergency path along the seaside road. Another slam of the door told her Nick had gotten out of the car.

"Faith," he called out, exasperated, "where do you think you're going?"

"Leave me alone, Nick Chandler," she muttered to herself. Fury spurred her on. She kept walking. The road was rocky, the asphalt chewed up by last winter's rain, but Faith stumbled along. Nick's footsteps behind her were growing louder. She sped up her pace.

One of her high-heeled shoes hit a rock and she tumbled forward onto the road. Nick's strong arms wound around her, enveloping her to safety just as a truck whizzed by. The driver blasted his horn. Nick lost his balance with her in his arms, and came up hard against a large boulder jutting out from the cliff side of the road. Bracing her, he took the brunt of the impact.

With their bodies plastered together on the now quiet highway, Nick ran a hand through her hair, gently cupping the back of her head. "That was not smart, Faith," he said when she lifted her eyes to his. Instead of anger, she saw a faint glimmer of warmth in those dark depths. Seconds ticked by.

He urged her closer, into his embrace. She went willingly, knowing all the while she shouldn't. Their thighs brushed together. "No, *this* is not smart," Faith replied with futility, because she couldn't conceive of stepping out of his arms.

"Don't I know it," he said softly, flashing her a look filled with confusion right before his lips came down on hers.

Faith had the willpower to fend off his kiss for all of three seconds before she succumbed to the remembered feel and taste of him. His lips slanted over hers firmly, taking possession, claiming them as his for this brief time. Unable to will her body to stop,

Faith moved closer so that their hips and thighs met. Nick groaned into her mouth, pressing his tongue inside. Faith too let out a small moan.

But the kiss ended abruptly when another car whizzed by. The toot of a horn brought her back to her senses. "That definitely shouldn't have happened," she grumbled, angry with herself. She lifted Nick's hands off her waist.

"Probably not," he agreed, looking equally angry with himself. But he reached for her hand and guided her back to his car.

Once seated in the car again, Faith couldn't look at him. He began, "Look, I'm sorry for what I said before. It was—"

"Crude?"

"All right, yes. Can you blame me?"

She shrugged, trying to sound nonchalant. "I guess not. But you don't know the half of it."

"Tell me."

"It doesn't matter, Nick. After tomorrow, we'll never have to see each other. Let's just try to get through the next two days. For Hope and Tony's sake."

"Is that the way you want it?"

"It's the way it has to be."

Nick started the engine without giving her a glance. Faith knew it would be months before she would forget the feel of having been in Nick Chandler's arms again.


"So, what did you think of Nick Chandler?" Hope asked, as she sipped the cup of coffee Faith had just set before her.

Faith slid into the seat facing her sister in their shared kitchen, realizing this would be the last night they'd spend together like this. After the wedding tomorrow, everything would change.

A stab of guilt sliced through Faith as she casually shrugged off Hope's question. She'd decided not to tell Hope anything about her encounter with Nick in Palm Springs until her sister returned from her honeymoon. No sense putting ideas in a master schemer's head. Besides, she wanted Hope to go away without a worry in the world, to have the time of her life. There would be time enough to discuss Faith's disastrous love life. "He's nice enough. Not my type."

"Did you get a good look at the man?" Hope asked incredulously. "He's every female's type."

After Nick's kiss this afternoon, she'd have to agree. Not too many women would resist his charm. Unfortunately, she had to count herself among them. "Hope, please."

"I know, I'm meddling again. But I keep wondering what took the two of you so long getting to the restaurant tonight." Hope's expectant expression gave her away. "Were you getting acquainted?"

Acquainted? Faith condemned herself at that moment and her stomach once again clenched. Nick Chandler had known every intimate inch of her. Known her as no other man ever had.

But Faith thought they'd gotten away with showing up late. She hadn't realized anyone in particular noticing how she and Nick slipped into the restaurant after everyone had already ordered their food. She'd considered herself fortunate. "Uh, well, Nick took a wrong turn."

That hadn't been far from the truth. The kiss should never have happened. Still, she hated deceiving her sister.

"You mean he couldn't find his way to Sandy Cove? He built that restaurant!"

"He did? I didn't realize he owned—"

"No, of course he doesn't own it, but Tony tells me that building that restaurant seven years ago is how Nick got started as an independent contractor. He's done very well for himself since then."

So what if he's successful, Faith thought. That didn't change the way she felt about him. Although, sitting alone in that bar last year, seeing such a handsome face looking so forlorn, so desolate, had Faith heading his way. His mysterious, hooded expression almost made her change her mind, almost made her turn from him. Those dark eyes had shuttered when he noticed her approach; but in those eyes, she'd also recognized the same despairing loneliness that was mirrored in her own. She'd felt inexplicably drawn to him.

"I guess we lingered a while at the church. He was concerned about my fall."

"Yeah, now that you mention it, Faith, why did you faint? Have you any idea? You're not the frail, delicate type. I've seen you handle much more stress than helping me with my wedding plans. What's going on?"

"Nothing that can't wait until you're back from your honeymoon. I'll explain then."

Hope's eyebrows shot up, and a worried frown pulled at her lips. "You're not sick?"

Faith took Hope's hand. "Heavens, no. Physically, I'm fine. Please believe me. There's absolutely nothing wrong with me. I wouldn't lie about that." But she would lie, had lied, about another subject. She wasn't really lying to her sister, just prolonging the truth, she rationalized. For Hope's benefit.

"I believe you. For now. But little sister, the minute I return from my honeymoon, I want a full report," she said with a grin. Faith and Hope had this running joke. While other fathers had asked for explanations from their daughters, their dad, a staunch Chicago police officer, had always asked for a *full report*.

When Hope, wild and uninhibited as a teen, would lead their father on a merry chase, Faith always opted to keep in line. She'd been dubbed a goody-two-shoes by her older sister. Faith never took risks as a child, and as an adult, nothing much had changed. Except for one crazy night in Palm Springs with a man she thought she'd never see again.

The irony was almost tangible. The one time Faith had dared to take a chance, it came back to torment her in the form of Nick Chandler.

"You'll get your full report. Now, forget about me. How are you doing? Nervous?"

"I've been waiting a lifetime for Tony DiMartino. He's perfect for me. I'm not nervous in the least."

Faith knew that would be her sister's answer. Hope had always been so sure of herself, even as a child. She knew what would make her happy and always went after it. A part of Faith envied her sister's tenacity, her confidence.

Faith had dated Peter Kaminsky for three years. Even after they were engaged, she still hadn't been entirely sure of her feelings. She had supposed he was the right one for her; she'd wanted him to be. Faith could see now, even though his deception devastated her at the time, that their breakup had been for the best. He was, after all, just Number One. And the magic of the charm always held true.

"Good. I think I'm more nervous for you. But not about Tony. I just want all the plans to go smoothly."

"They will," Hope offered.

"It's late. You need your beauty sleep," Faith said with a wink. "I'll clean up. You have a big day tomorrow."

"Thanks, sis." Hope gave Faith a giant bear hug and said good night.

Morning dawned cloudy, lending a gloominess to what should be a wonderful day. But summer mornings in the inland town were always overcast and cool. An ocean breeze from just over the canyon would never fail to kick up in the afternoon, blowing away the threatening gray puffs and leaving the air somewhat warmer.

Faith peered out the window to see the persistent California sun peeking through the clouds. She showered and dressed early in anticipation of the day's events.

The off-the-shoulder soft pink velvet dress Faith wore as the maid of honor was certainly much less revealing than the emerald green one of the night before. With her hair held back in a French twist and absolutely no cleavage exposed, Faith felt more like herself. She gave herself a nod of approval, smiled into the mirror, then twirled around in the floor-length gown she deemed perfect for a late summer wedding. This was the real Faith McAllister, whether Nick Chandler believed her or not.

Last night during the rehearsal dinner, Faith hadn't found it hard to steer clear of him. She chose a seat furthest away from his and paid no attention to him. By night's end, she'd had three other offers to drive her back to the church to retrieve her car.

She'd accepted a ride from Debra Brayley, an old college friend of Hope's, one of the three brides-maids. The recently divorced woman pumped her for information about Nick Chandler throughout the twenty minute drive. By the time Faith reached the church, she'd been sick of hearing about the eye con-tact Debra made with the man, how gloriously hand-some she thought he was and how much she'd love to know everything about him. Faith couldn't wait to get out from the suffocating woman's inquisition. Talk about desperation.

Faith knew that if she could only keep a good dis-tance from Nick throughout the festivities, she'd never have to lay eyes on him again. Determined to have a wonderful time, she vowed not to let Nick spoil the day.

She knocked on Hope's door and called out, "All set in there?"

"Come in. I need reinforcements." Faith entered her sister's room. The sight of Hope dressed in white satin took her breath away. "Oh, Hope, you look stun-ning."

"Thanks," she said with a glowing smile. "Could you help me do up these buttons?" Hope asked, ges-turing to her back.

Faith finished buttoning her sister's gown.

"You look lovely too," her sister went on. "How's your head feeling this morning?"

"The bump is almost gone. I feel wonderful. Not to worry."

"Okay, I won't. Oh, and I forgot to tell you last night, Nick won't be riding in the limo with us to the church."

That suited Faith just fine. "That's not a problem.

He has obligations to Tony. Is he giving the anxious groom a lift?"

"No, Tony said he was picking up a date. But you know how Tony loves to torment me, he wouldn't tell me her name. Sorry, sis. I had hoped that Nick would be your escort today."

Faith told herself she was glad. Having Nick focus attention on his date would make it easier for her to dodge him. So why did her heart jolt at the thought of seeing another woman on his arm? "Nothing to be sorry about."

But Faith was sorry.

Sorry she'd ever met Nick Chandler in the first place.

Faith watched as Nick whirled his date around the dance floor with fluid, confident movements. All eyes in the reception hall were on them. His date turned out to be Mary DiMartino, Tony's mother. The gray-haired woman threw her head back and laughed at something Nick said. With obvious affection, Nick's mouth quirked up, flashing the woman a charming grin.

Faith averted her gaze, afraid she'd be caught eyeing the handsome man. She didn't want to notice him, but how could she not? Looking roguish in his tuxedo, she'd never laid eyes on a more sexy man. He oozed sensuality with each smile, each sharp, well-honed gaze. And every other female in the room seemed to be ogling him too, including Debra, who sat beside Faith and made little throaty sounds as her gaze shamelessly followed his every move. Irritated, Faith got up from her seat and headed for the ladies room.

Nick caught up to her before she reached the door. "I guess we have to do this."

Startled, Faith looked into his eyes with question. "Do what?"

He gestured to the dance floor with a jerk of his head. "They're calling for the bridal party."

"Oh," Faith said, watching the bridesmaids being led by their counterparts to the center of the parquet floor. "I guess we do."

Nick didn't touch her until they faced each other on the floor. The band began playing a soft, melodic tune. Faith stiffened when he took her in his arms. Nick noticed and anger flashed in those dark, brooding eyes for one moment. "Relax, Irish, it's only a dance. No need to take it so seriously."

Faith let her stiffened shoulders down slowly. "I don't know what you mean."

Nick chuckled, low and deep in her ear. "Sure you do."

No sense arguing, the man was cocky to a fault and too confident for his own good. Just a few more hours, Faith reminded herself, and then this nightmare would be over.

Faith commanded her body to relax in his arms; although where he was concerned, she would never let down her guard. She felt Nick's hands leisurely roam down her side to the small of her back, drawing her closer. She had no choice but to wind her arms around his neck, but managed to keep a decent distance away without being too obvious. His fingers traced the expanse of her waist and he applied a slight pressure. She made no comment.

"You've put on a few pounds," he whispered in her ear.

"Have not," she defended, even though she knew she had. After the breakup with Peter, she hadn't eaten for days. In fact, it had taken her weeks to regain some semblance of an appetite. She knew she'd lost weight at that time, and, since Nick had known her, she had regained some of those pounds.

"Don't get testy, it looks good on you."

"Oh," she said, unprepared for the compliment. She had no reason to expect one kind word from this man.

"Not that you weren't an eyeful when we met. You caught my attention without having to bat an eyelash. The flashy hair, the long legs, that damned dress." He squeezed her again, a bit harder this time, but not to inflict pain, she surmised, only humiliation. And he was doing quite well.

"Shhh!" she whispered, glancing at the others on the dance floor, hoping no one would hear. "Please, Nick. Just drop it."

He gave her a look with a sharp tilt of his head that said he was not willing to drop it.

"I need some air." Faith stopped dancing and moved out of his grasp. She turned toward the double doors leading to the garden. The grounds of the Los Angeles Country Club were immaculately groomed, beautifully landscaped. She stopped once she reached a small wooden bridge. Resting her arms on the white railing, she took a deep breath of fresh air.

She wanted so much for this night to be over. Nick had just begun his torment. What he hoped to gain, she hadn't a clue. Except, knowing male pride, she assumed he had been furious to find her gone that morning in Palm Springs. She'd probably bruised his masculine ego, being the one to walk away first. It hadn't been her intent to hurt anyone. If she'd had the courage she'd have stayed to face him, to apologize.

Apologize?

For the most satisfying night of her life? No, she wouldn't have apologized exactly; she simply would have tried to explain to him why she'd behaved that way, made him see she hadn't planned on—planned on what?

Feeling something.

That night had been a confused, jumbled-up mess of emotions. But she *had* felt something, and it scared her. She was on the rebound, in a major way. It had been too soon. She had known nothing about him. He would have walked away anyway, wouldn't he have?

"You really are beautiful, here, in the moonlight." Nick's husky voice cut into her thoughts. She didn't turn to face him. He stood on the bridge next to her, looking out.

"I'm waiting," she said impatiently after a long moment of silence.

"For what?"

His eyes were on her now. She felt the heat of his gaze, but didn't dare look at him. "For the other shoe to drop."

He laughed, a small laugh that told her she'd amused him. "I guess I deserve that."

Surprised at his light mood, she looked into his eyes, at his smile. When his features weren't hardened by whatever had caused the anguish in his life, he was quite incredible. Dangerously so.

She remembered that as well.

"Yes, Nick, you did deserve that. I've looked forward to this day for a long time. I want nothing to spoil my sister's wedding."

"I won't spoil it for Tony, either. So we're even."

"If your compliment was real, this time, I'll say thank you and ask you to leave me for a few minutes. I need . . . time." The words came out shaky. Hardly the confident woman she'd pretended to be in Palm Springs.

"It *was* real, and I'm afraid I can't do that. They're calling for the toast."

"Oh, well, in that case we'd better go in."

Faith lifted her gown and made a move to brush past him. He caught her arm in a swift move. She fastened her gaze to his fingers pressing gently into her upper arm. They were warm and gentle this time, almost a caress. "I'd like to call a truce for tonight, Faith."

For tonight? Judging that she'd have to suffer his company for another few hours, she was ecstatic. If he really meant it. She knew how important Tony's friendship was to him. Nick had probably decided to put aside what had happened between them last year in order to assure a happy ending to a perfect wedding. She searched his eyes. "Why?"

"Why else?" The slight tilt of his head toward the reception hall answered her question. Faith wondered if he had another motive, but she decided to give him the benefit of the doubt. This one time.

"I'd like that," she responded softly. "And after tonight, we're not likely to run into each other again."

He neither agreed, nor disagreed, but the smallest flicker in his unfathomable eyes made Faith uneasy the rest of the night.

# THREE

With the wedding reception over, Faith decided keeping busy was better than reminiscing about times shared in the condo she and Hope had occupied all these years. She'd taken it upon herself to see to Hope and Tony's wedding gifts. Refusing further help from Tony's brothers, she said her goodbyes on the small road by the country club's entrance, thanking them heartily for loading up her car.

Once outside her condo, she parked the car and lifted the hood. Removing a large silver-foiled square gift box, as well as two smaller ones, she began her trek up the few steps from the parking lot through the garden, up another round of steps, to finally reach her door. The gifts were plentiful, and so artistically wrapped that Faith made a game of guessing what was in each box. "Coffee maker for sure, or my name's not Faith Heather McAllister."

By her third trip from the car, she'd guessed three coffee makers, two toasters and at least four sets of towels. One couldn't have enough good towels, she mused.

More than once, she caught herself glancing at the notecards, wondering which gift had come from Nick. She couldn't understand why she'd felt so desolate this evening after they'd said a rather quick good-bye to each other. In her mind, she knew not seeing him again would be wise, but in her heart . . .

No. She couldn't let herself imagine having a relationship with the man, not that he'd offered. After their truce in the garden, Nick Chandler had avoided her with expert care. He'd danced with Tony's mother again, then Debra finally got her claws into him.

Although, Faith admitted wryly, he didn't seem at all taken by Debra. Cold and aloof were the best words to describe how he'd treated her. Not that Debra had noticed. Her eyes had sparkled with something akin to wonderment as Nick turned her around the dance floor. Nick had looked bored, and Faith had mentally chided herself for being relieved.

"Quit thinking about Nick Chandler," she admonished herself rather loudly, then chuckled.

With arms loaded, she sped up her pace. A sprinkler head seemed to come out of nowhere to trip her up. She landed with a thud on the lawn, and all three packages went flying high in the air before landing in the grass. "Good going," she muttered." I hope nothing's broken." She sat on the moonlit lawn, summoning the will to get up, realizing the futility of her helpful gesture. All these gifts would eventually have to be moved to Tony's house once the newly married couple came home from their honeymoon in Jamaica.

Faith would be moving into their home tomorrow, to dog sit, house sit and have a well-deserved vacation of her own. She might as well unload the gifts then. With a groan, she retraced her steps and began load-

ing the wedding presents back into the trunk of her
car.

Faith looked forward to getting a little rest and
recreation while helping her sister and new brother-
in-law by looking after the house. And Hope had
assured her that Tony would be relieved his three-
year-old beagle, Legal, would have a companion.
Faith had timed some renovations on her condo for
the day Hope was leaving on her honeymoon, so
without too much arm twisting, Faith had agreed.

And it sounded like heaven.

Tony's home was a sprawling four bedroom tri-level
built on a cliff that overlooked the Pacific Ocean.
Both Hope and Faith loved the location as much as
they admired the modern, open-air feel to the home.
Faith was to enjoy herself, making full use of the pool,
the spa and the sauna. She saw no problem with that
in the least.

Once finished replacing the gifts in her trunk,
Faith let out a giant sigh. She was bone-tired. And
fainting the other day hadn't helped matters any.
With the wedding going off beautifully, the honey-
mooners off to a romantic destination and Nick
Chandler out of her life for good, Faith could finally
get a good night's sleep. With that in mind, she un-
dressed, showered and climbed into her bed.

The last thing she remembered as she lowered her
eyelids was an image of Nick Chandler, with unread-
able eyes and looking more tempting than sin itself
dressed in his black tuxedo, giving her a chaste kiss
on the cheek before saying goodbye.


She didn't take too much to Tony's house, just a
large overnight duffel and a bag of books she in-

tended to read while she lolled by the pool. It was mid-September and one could always count on heat, as well as high humidity at this time of year. She packed shorts and more shorts, throwing in several summer dresses and a few swimsuits. She smiled at the thought that she was finally on vacation. And even though she was only going to be thirty minutes away from her condo, she felt as if she'd entered another world.

Malibu.

It wasn't her style, but hey, no one had to know that.

She could relax, kick back and unwind, as soon as she rid herself of all these darned gifts.

She glanced at the packages in her arms and groaned. If familiarity breeds contempt, then she'd have to agree. She was getting far too familiar with these gifts. Why, she could spot the coffee maker at twenty paces!

Anxious to relieve herself of her burden, she put the packages down and jingled the key ring in her right hand until she found the one Hope had given her last night. With the door unlocked, Faith let out a tiny sigh of relief, picked up the gifts and entered the house.

A sharp noise startled her. She jumped back, slamming her backside into the front door she'd just closed. "Ouch!" she said in a strained whisper. Another banging noise, then another, bombarded her eardrums. It sounded like the house was crumbling.

Earthquake!

No. She'd lived through two of L.A.'s terrible tremors so she knew the clues. There was no grumbling under her feet. No room fixtures swinging. No walls vibrating. Just noise. Earth-shattering banging, coming from the lower level, so it seemed.

Then it occurred to her that she was not alone. Someone else was in the house. Destroying the house. Burglars? Or worse?

Faith was no fool. She knew enough to get out, and do it quickly and quietly, before she was discovered. But what of Tony and Hope's home? She backed out of the front door, setting down the gifts and leaving all her belongings on the front porch. This was no time to worry about her clothes. She had to get to her car and call for help.

There was no way to silently start her motor. Once the engine roared to life, her little white Honda took off and headed down the hill. Then she remembered her cellular phone. Of course! She kept it in the glove compartment of the car to use in case of emergencies. She pulled the car to a stop and whipped out the phone, dialing 911.

"I'd like to report a burglary or something. I don't know exactly what's going on in the house, but there's terrible noise and no one's supposed to be in there."

The police dispatcher told her to stay out of sight and wait until the police arrived. They would send a unit immediately to the address given.

Faith used the cellular phone again, this time to place a call to her Uncle Joe. He wasn't really a relation, but he'd been her father's best friend at the precinct back east for twenty years and he lived just minutes from here. She and Hope had always referred to him as their uncle. Retired now, he'd spent the last years of his police career working as a captain with the LAPD.

With Hope gone, Uncle Joe would give her the moral support she needed. Her legs shook and her stomach knotted, realizing what awful fate might have befallen her in the hands of whoever was in that house minutes ago.

"Uncle Joe, this is Faith. I'm afraid something's happening over at Hope and Tony's. I had just arrived when I heard loud banging noises. Someone's in there. I just called 911."

"Where are you now?"

"I'm in my car, just down the hill. I need to stay here until they catch whoever it is."

"Just keep yourself safe, will you, girl? I'll come over right away."

"Oh no, Uncle Joe. I didn't mean for you to come. I just needed, well, a friendly voice. That's all."

"And you'll have one. In the flesh, dearie. Now, give your uncle the address. I'll find out what I can. Stay put."

Faith gave her uncle all the information, then slouched in the seat of her car to wait. She never heard sirens, but she assumed the police wouldn't want to alert the intruder. Exactly fifteen minutes later—Faith had been counting—a uniformed officer approached her car. "Miss McAllister?"

"Yes."

"I'm Officer Benton. You called in a burglary?"

"Uh-huh. Did you catch the thieves?"

"Well, now, you'll have to come with me. We'll have to clear this up. There might be a misunderstanding."

Faith got out of her car slowly. "Misunderstanding? Now, I don't understand."

"Come along, please. You'll need to answer a few

questions, make an identification." The officer took huge strides. Faith had to jog just to keep up with the long-legged man.

"I never got a look at him."

"Maybe not, but he says he knows you." Officer Benton twisted his lips up ruefully. "And he's not a happy man."

"I don't care about the disposition of a would-be criminal, Officer."

"Oh, I think you'll care about this one."

Faith stopped once they reached the driveway leading to the house. It was silly for her to be fearful. There were four uniformed officers, all surrounding the man in question. Even Uncle Joe was there and he was grinning from ear to ear.

Faith had a queasy feeling, as if she'd been punched in the gut and the turmoil roiled around wildly, wickedly. Something was not right.

A sea of black uniforms parted slightly, and all heads turned in her direction. The quartet of officers had amused looks on their faces, but the man who was just now having his handcuffs removed was not smiling, not at all happy, and was most definitely . . . Nick Chandler.

"Nick!"

Nick glared.

Faith froze.

Uncle Joe smiled.

Officer Benton took Faith by the arm and escorted her toward the huddled group. "This man claims to be Nick Chandler. He's working on the DiMartino house while they're away. Do you know this man, miss?"

Dumbfounded, Faith nodded.

"I've confirmed it, dear girl." Uncle Joe kissed her forehead. "I didn't think I'd see you again so soon after the wedding. I do remember Hope introducing me to the best man yesterday. I remarked on what a handsome couple the two of you made."

*Not now, Uncle Joe. Please.* Faith felt herself withering.

Officer Benton chimed in, "He's got no paperwork, nothing that supports his claim that he's working here. No contract."

Confused, Faith shook her head. "I didn't know he'd be here. But he's who he says he is."

Faith dared to glance at Nick, who was rubbing his wrists where he'd been handcuffed. His lips were set in a thin line. Anger sparked from his deep-set eyes and his expression could only be described as grim.

Faith groaned silently. She felt like the Wicked Witch of the North and wished that she, too, could melt away right on the spot.

"I've already explained everything. Tony and Hope are friends of mine. I'm doing work on their house. I have a key," Nick said quietly to Uncle Joe.

"They knew you'd be coming? They actually gave you a key?" Faith's tirade ended when Nick glared at her.

Faith threw her arms around herself and began to pace. "Well, those two schemers! Wait until I see them again!"

"Uh, Miss McAllister. We'll be heading out now. Joe Rooney's word is as good as gold. It seems this was all a big misunderstanding. Everything Mr. Chandler told us about himself seems to check out. Unless you want to file a complaint or—"

"Oh, no, no. That won't be necessary. It was just an innocent . . . mistake." *I've been tricked, duped,* she didn't say. *Hope is going to pay for this one.*

"Well, our apologies, Mr. Chandler."

Nick nodded, apparently not angry with the police. He was, though, furious with her, if the distinct flaring of his nostrils and narrowing of his eyes were any indication.

She watched Uncle Joe shake Nick's hand, pat him firmly on the back and turn to her to say goodbye. Faith must have looked wretched, because Uncle Joe brought his fist to her chin and gently cuffed her. It was a reminder of her childhood. When she'd gotten in trouble with her parents, Uncle Joe had always given her an encouraging word. This time, he said, "I'll be leaving now, girl. I don't want to be around for the fireworks." He chuckled, darting his gaze from her to Nick.

"Thanks for coming," Faith said dejectedly.

Uncle Joe winked and left the two of them standing alone in the front yard. Abruptly, Nick turned on his heel and strode through the front doors. Faith followed.

In the kitchen, Nick pulled a beer from the refrigerator and slugged down half the bottle before Faith caught up with him. She drew in a deep breath. "I suppose you hate me."

Silence.

"I am very sorry. But you see, I didn't know you'd be here. And the banging sounded so awful. What were you doing, anyway?"

Silence.

Nick stared out the window.

"If you have to be mad, be mad at Tony and Hope. They set us up."

"I knew you'd be coming," he said flatly.

Stunned, Faith took a moment to let that register. "What?"

Nick turned to her. "I said, I knew you'd show up."

"How?"

"Your sister told me she'd given you the key, and if I wanted to stop by sometime, it'd be all right."

"The rat." Faith took a step closer. "So you decided to bang up the house?"

Nick's look was fierce. He said through gritted teeth, "Tony wanted to surprise Hope with a new home office. I offered to do the work as my wedding gift to them."

Parts of the puzzle were beginning to come together. Hope had often wished she and Tony could spend more hours together. Both being busy professionals in the real estate business, a home office would ensure them more down time. "So you couldn't very well spoil the surprise by telling Hope that you'd be here working on a new room for her."

"Not new, I'm converting the room next to the den downstairs. But, yeah, that's exactly right."

Faith nodded. "But now that I'm here, you'll just have to finish it later."

"Nope." His expression was set.

Faith cringed. "What do you mean, no? I'm house sitting. I'm dog sitting. I've taken a two-week vacation."

He shrugged. "Vacation somewhere else. I'll watch the house and the dog. Where is Legal, anyway?"

Faith ignored his question. She was too distressed

about this turn of events. "I can't vacation anywhere but here. I have no place else to go!"

"Go home, Faith. The sooner, the better. I have work to do."

"Well, I don't. I can't go home. You'll just have to do your work another time."

Nick slammed the beer bottle down on the table and came to stand dangerously close to her. He looked down with a snarl twisting his lips. "Tony is the best—correction, only—real friend I have. I will not go back on my word. He expects a new room for your sister, his bride, when they return and damn it, he'll get one. And you can just leave right now if you don't like it."

The truce of last night was definitely over. If he'd slapped her, the sting wouldn't have hurt as much. Now, she knew exactly how he felt about her. "Believe me, I wish I could. But you see, my condo is being fumigated tomorrow, then the painters come and after that, the new carpet will be installed. I can't possibly go home."

"Cancel them, do it another time! That's what you're asking me to do. Only I don't run out on people when I give my word. You apparently do."

Faith put her hands on her hips. He'd insulted her one too many times today. And what did he mean with that crack about her running out on people? He didn't know her well enough to condemn her that way. Certainly, he couldn't be referring to the night in Palm Springs. They had both known going in what the end result of that would be, *had* to be. They both knew they'd pay the price in the morning for their night of passion.

Granted, he did have a right to be angry about his

near arrest, but that really wasn't all her fault. He hadn't mentioned a word about it. She thought he'd taken her innocent mistake quite well.

She couldn't reschedule all the workmen at her place. It had taken her two months to coordinate everything, and she'd gotten the best prices available. She couldn't afford to cancel now, to pay a higher price later, nor did she have any more vacation time coming this year. To cancel would mean having to wait another year.

No. Canceling wasn't an option. Faith began to consider an idea that popped into her head. It wasn't an ideal solution, but at least some part of her vacation would be salvaged.

She chose to ignore his insults for now. "Nick, we could work out a compromise, couldn't we?"

"What kind of compromise?" He backed off slightly, even looked interested.

"Well, maybe you could come to work here in the mornings. I'm an early riser. I'll jog down by the beach or take long walks, run errands. We won't really have to see each other at all. The afternoon and evenings will be mine."

He was silent for a moment, thoughtful, then his expression changed. "And you think that's a good compromise?"

Yes, she thought so. Why was he smirking? "We're both between a rock and a hard place, I'll admit. But yes, I do think it's a decent solution."

"Not from where I stand."

"Why not?"

He smiled then, and it nearly took her breath away. "You don't know, do you?"

Faith was losing her patience. Only the thrill of

seeing him finally smile, flashing straight white teeth, kept her from losing it altogether. Her vacation was as good as ruined, but at least the work on the condo she'd been planning for months would get accomplished. "Know what, Nick?"

Nick rubbed a palm over his face, contemplated, then cast her an intensely sexy look. His eyes raked over her body and, for the first time, she remembered how she was dressed. She wore denim cut-offs with more holes in them than Swiss cheese and a thin-ribbed tank top that was two sizes too small. The only thing about her that remotely resembled Faith McAllister, librarian, was the bun knotted at the top of her head. And even that wasn't cooperating because the knot had come loose and most of her hair had fallen down around her face. Well, she hadn't planned on seeing anyone today, much less Nick.

"I know you really didn't expect anyone to be here today," he finally replied.

"No. I didn't. I wouldn't have called the police if I had."

His eyes were hard, but his touch was gentle when he stroked her cheek. "Maybe we could work out a compromise." He shrugged. "Of sorts."

Faith knew just what kind of compromise he meant. He was trying to scare her. But she didn't scare that easily. In fact, she felt a tingle down to her toes at his suggestion.

Nick's eyes danced in wicked amusement. And his grin was deadly. "Tony gave me carte blanche to use his place while he's gone. I'll be living here for the next two weeks."

"You can't be serious!" she shrieked. "Hope wouldn't do this to me. She just wouldn't."

"Who knows, with all the wedding commotion, they may have forgotten to confide in each other. Tony certainly wouldn't want to ruin your sister's surprise. Then again . . ."

A shudder rippled through Faith's body when she realized that Nick may have told Tony all about their one night affair. "You didn't tell Tony—I mean he doesn't know about us. That isn't what this is all about?"

"Ah, Faith, you wound me. Everyone knows a gentleman doesn't kiss and tell. Don't worry, your adoring brother-in-law stills thinks you're as pure as the driven snow. And I'm sure a proper little librarian like you hasn't owned up to your sister either."

"No, I haven't." She scoffed at his reference to being a gentleman. He was enjoying her anguish all too much. And she did plan on explaining everything to Hope sometime in the future.

"Okay, then, it's settled. You're leaving," he said in a commanding tone.

"Why do I have to be the one to go?"

When he scowled, Faith knew she had tested his patience. But, she wasn't prepared for him to reach out and circle her waist with his arms. Nick drew her close with a no-nonsense look on his face and suddenly Faith became wary. Roughly cupping her head in his hand, he brought his mouth down on hers hard. His lips bruised hers and she stiffened.

A tiny moan escaped her throat. His kiss became more potent, more demanding. Taking her closer in his embrace, he plied her lips open and stroked her tongue with his. Fire shot up inside her, and an awareness of all that was male, all that was appealing, all that was dangerous about Nick Chandler stole over her.

Faith knew she should pull away, but his lips on hers had become more gentle, and his fingers threaded through her hair now with tenderness. Instead of pushing him away, she grasped the open collar of his work shirt and tugged him nearer. He made a deep-throated groan, then angled his body to hers so their bodies meshed. Faith brought her hands up to circle his neck.

At that moment, she felt Nick grow still. He swore and abruptly broke off the kiss. A glimmer of regret flashed in his eyes before they turned cold, unyielding. "That's why you have to go, Faith. Leave now, because I'm staying."

Faith fingered her swollen lips and quieted her trembling body. Sometime during that kiss, this had become war. She was angry at having allowed him to coax such a heated response from her. She made up her mind—she would not let Nick bully her out of her vacation: "I'm not leaving either. So, if you'd kindly promise not to do that again, I'll stay out of your way. And you'll stay out of mine."

Nick stared at her for a long moment. He scratched his chin thoughtfully. "I promise," he said finally. Relieved she'd won the first battle, she smiled until she heard him add, "I promise to try. But I make no guarantees, Irish. So if you stay, it'll be at your own risk."

Darn him anyway, he wouldn't budge an inch. Okay, at least she knew what she was up against. She considered herself forewarned.

A slight burning sensation just underneath her Triple Charm bracelet made her glance down quickly.

Sunlight sparkled on the second charm, making it look iridescent, while the others remained the same gilded color. The heat from that charm almost scorched her skin. Instinctively, she flicked her wrist. Both the burning and the glow vanished. She blinked, sure she'd imagined the whole thing, then looked up at an expectant Nick. "I—I'm staying . . . at my own risk."

She turned to retrieve her luggage and settle in.

This vacation would be one for the books.

# FOUR

"Where should I sleep?" Faith asked, hoisting her duffel bag over her shoulder.

Nick grinned. "Is this a trick question?"

Judging by the frown on her face, Faith didn't find his teasing amusing. "It's obvious you've already moved in, but I want to be out of your way. As far as possible."

Nick unburdened Faith of her duffel bag and picked up her other bag, leading the way. "I'm afraid I can't put you too far away. You can take the master bedroom. I'm in the room next door." They climbed the spiral staircase. "The last room on this floor has a single bed. Too small for me."

"Then I'll take it."

He stopped on the step above her and turned. "Look, either way, we'll be next to each other. You may as well have the king-sized bed. You'll have your own bath and lots of privacy." Nick turned and began climbing again.

"What about the guest room downstairs? One of us could take that."

"That's the room I'm converting. It's next to the den on the lower level. I've already knocked out a wall."

"That's the racket I heard earlier."

"Yeah. But my work usually doesn't get me arrested." He stopped to look at her once they reached the top of the stairs.

"I said I was sorry. How was I to know you'd be here? I didn't see your car."

"My truck's parked around back." He rubbed his jaw. "Man, when they put those cuffs on me, suddenly I felt like a teenager again."

"You've been arrested before?"

Her tone, the look of stunned surprise on Faith's face, hurt. He lifted one corner of his mouth. "Detained—for shoplifting—grand theft auto, among other things," he said ruefully. "I haven't always been a model citizen, Faith. Maybe you want to change your mind about living with me for the next two weeks."

Nick had to give her credit. He noted a fleeting moment of indecision, then she looked him square in the eye. "I won't exactly be living with you, Nick. We'll be sharing a residence. And besides, you have work to do. I'm on vacation. Our paths won't cross too much. It's a big house."

She seemed to have convinced herself. He nodded. "Your call."

When they reached the master suite, Nick gave a shove to open the door, and set her luggage down. "Make yourself at home."

Faith looked into the large rectangular room. Sunlight streamed in from wall to wall windows. The deep blue waters of the Pacific in the distance encompassed the entire length of the room, making the scene look like some incredible wall mural. "This view is magnificent. I had no idea. I've never been up here."

The wistful look on her face gave him intense pleasure. Nick wondered if she knew he built this house. "You mean Tony never put the moves on you?"

She turned from the view. "Tony? Of course not, I'm not his type. Hope's so much more—"

Nick interrupted, "Just kidding, Faith. Tony's as true blue as they come. And don't be so quick to put yourself down. I'm sure if Tony had met you first—"

"Nothing would have come of it. As I said, I'm not his type."

Like hell. Nick knew Tony like a brother, better than a brother. And any man who knew women could see through Faith's meek librarian facade. She was fooling herself, but Nick knew better. He had witnessed her passion at firsthand; once unleashed, she was a female dynamo.

Thinking of leashes, he was reminded of the missing canine. Letting the other conversation drop, he changed the subject. "Where's the dog?"

"Huh? Oh! Legal Beagle. I almost forgot. Hope left me directions to pick him up." She rummaged through her bag and found a note. "Here it is. The address is on Rosemont Drive. I remember her saying Tony's mother has him."

"That's her address. I'll get him."

"No, I will. It's my responsibility. You have work to do, remember?"

Nick sighed. He'd never met such a stubborn woman. "Listen, I'll drive you. Mrs. DiMartino has something for me. I had intended to go over there anyway. No sense in both of us driving. Besides, Legal can be a handful in the car. Damn dog'll be all over you."

"Fine, just give me a few minutes to unpack and change my clothes."

"I'll be downstairs. Take your time." Nick turned and walked away.

Finally alone, Faith marveled again at the beautiful ocean view she would enjoy for the next two weeks. The huge bedroom seemed larger than the condo she had shared with Hope.

Unlike many austere-looking master suites, this one had a certain homey warmth. There was a small sitting area which faced a smooth-tiled fireplace. The wing chairs looked cozy. Faith thought of all the reading she'd do here late at night, with the French doors to the balcony open, letting in the sea breezes to cool the room's heat.

The bathroom was enormous, a sunken tub on one end and a double-sized stall shower on the other. There were two sinks, two walk-in closets and a dressing table. His and hers. These rooms were better than any hotel accommodations she'd ever had.

She glanced at her reflection in the mirror and realized she was in need of repairs. She definitely had to change the tattered shirt and worn-out shorts; Faith normally didn't dress this way. And she had to get her hair back up into its bun. Too bad there wasn't time for a shower, but even though Nick had told her to take her time, she doubted he was the patient type.

She knew he wasn't the patient type. He'd been an impatient lover, moving quickly, stealthily over her body, making sure each intimate part of her body was cherished fully with his lips, his hands.

He hadn't given her time to think. Perhaps he knew if he had, she would have bolted and run before they began their one night affair. But Nick had been generous to her needs, and she had returned his fervor with a boldness that to this day she could still not believe.

Momentary madness.

She had no other excuse.

She lifted the clothes out of her duffel bag and set them gently onto the bed. Donning a modestly cut light green short set, she viewed herself in the mirror. With her hair tightly secured on top of her head and her clothes properly in place, she felt like herself again.

She was going to enjoy this vacation. And she wouldn't let anyone, especially Nick Chandler, get in her way.


When Faith and Nick arrived at the DiMartino house, Tony's pleasantly plump mother, Mary, ushered them in and sat them down in the kitchen. Before Faith could blink her eyes, the kind-hearted woman had served up the best plate of pasta she had ever eaten. Small wonder why Nick insisted on coming here. He quickly ate two servings and started in on a dish of sausages and meatballs.

"I don't know how I'm ever going to get any work done today. I'm about to explode. You still make a mean fusilli, Mrs. D," Nick said with affection. If he had called her "Mom," it wouldn't have been more loving.

"You still love my cooking, Nicky? I missed feeding you while you were gone. Just because you're all grown up doesn't mean you can't come around for a plate of pasta. This is still your home. You come anytime. And bring Hope's sister."

Nick gave her a sideways glance. Faith shifted in her seat. Why did everyone assume they were a couple? "Thank you, Mrs. DiMartino."

"You call me Mary, please. You like the pasta?"

"Oh, yes. It's delicious."

The older woman nodded. "I made cannolis. And espresso." She wiped her hands on her apron. "I'll get them."

Faith wanted to protest. She couldn't eat another bite, but she didn't want to hurt the woman's feelings. Faith stood and picked up her plate. "May I help clear the dishes?"

Mary rushed over to her, taking the plate out of Faith's hands. "No, no. You sit with Nicky. Relax. I don't need help."

Faith sank back down in her seat. She turned when she heard Nick chuckle. "What's so funny?"

"Mrs. D doesn't take no for an answer, so just grin and bear it."

Faith put her hands over her stomach and groaned. "But I don't think I can eat another bite."

"You don't want to insult her. Just pass me whatever you can't eat when she's not looking. Works every time."

"You've done that before?"

"Sure. With Tony, Matt and Louie. It was like a game. When Mrs. D wasn't looking, suddenly one of us would find something on our plate that wasn't there before and, unless we found a way to put it back where it belonged, we had to eat it. The consequences were even worse and we all knew it."

"Why? That sweet woman couldn't possibly intimidate the likes of Tony and his brothers."

"No, but if you didn't feel like eating, she immediately thought you were sick. She'd feel your head for fever, ask about a hundred questions and dote on you the rest of the day. It was just easier to eat."

Faith nodded. "Must have been fun living with all of them."

"I didn't," he said after taking a sip of soda.

Surprised, Faith said, "But I assumed—I mean, from what you'd said I thought at some point in your life you lived here."

"I spent a lot of time here. Days at a time. But I always had to go back. I lived with my father. John Chandler was a falling-down drunk. I hated going home, if anyone could call that shack a home."

"I see."

"I don't think you do, but it doesn't matter."

Faith stared at Nick. His voice took on a bitter edge and his dark eyes looked cold. But warmth flooded into them when he viewed Mary coming back from the kitchen loaded down with a tray of Italian pastries and a set of small espresso cups. He rose and lifted the tray from her arms. "I've got it. Now sit down, Mrs. D. I'll serve.

The woman sat down and smiled at Faith. "I let my boys boss me around once in a while. Makes them feel like men." She winked.

Faith laughed and was overwhelmed with emotion when Nick bent down and placed a kiss on Mary's chubby cheek. She patted his arm. "And I had the best looking date for Tony and Hope's wedding."

"Ah, Mrs. D, you flatterer." Nick finished pouring the coffee and sat down next to Faith.

Mary turned to Faith, her face beaming with pride. "Nicky always promised when Tony got married, he'd pick me up and drive me to the church himself. And that boy didn't forget." Mary cast a look of adoration Nick's way.

"A promise is a promise." Nick grabbed two cannolis, placing one on Faith's plate and one on his own. His eyes twinkled in amusement when he glanced at Faith. "These look great. You make them today?"

"This morning. That dog kept trying to jump up on the table to see what I was doing. I put him outside. I know Tony spoils the dog but I don't like him in my kitchen."

"We'll take him off your hands, Mary," Faith said, taking a tiny bite of the pastry and declaring it wonderful.

"I don't mind doing Hope and Tony a favor, but I will be glad when he's gone. You said *we?*" Mary's eyes darted from Faith to Nick's.

Faith stiffened and realized her blunder. Now she'd have to explain to Mary about her temporary living arrangement with Nick.

Nick cleared his throat. "It's a long story. We'll be taking turns watching the dog. You said you had something for me, Mrs. D?"

Nick continued to surprise Faith. Was he covering for her, knowing that telling Mary the details of their living arrangements made Faith uncomfortable, or did he want to spare himself Mary's inevitable questions? Mary DiMartino was definitely not a woman of the nineties. She would not approve. Hope had often said that Tony had come from a very old-fashioned family and Faith could see that having Mary's respect and approval meant a great deal to Nick.

"Oh, yes. I have it right here." Mary got up and shuffled through a pile of mail on her kitchen counter. When the unsuspecting woman turned her back, Nick grabbed Faith's cannoli and stuffed it into his mouth. He chewed fast and had no trouble swallowing it before she returned.

Faith stifled a chuckle by coughing.

Mary walked over to Nick, keeping her eyes focused on the piece of mail she was holding. Then she set the unopened letter down right in front of him. "It's from your mother. I think you should open it this time," she said encouragingly, then squeezed his shoulders affectionately before sitting down.

Nick frowned, staring down at the beautiful white parchment envelope. "The woman's got impeccable taste, I'll say that for her." He shoved the letter into his shirt pocket. "I'll think about it."

Mary's eyes filled with compassion and she let out a low sigh. "Nicky—"

"We really should be going. Point me to Legal and I'll get him out of your way."

"He's in the backyard. You know the way." Mary tried to keep the disappointment out of her voice, but Faith picked up on it. And from the way Nick averted his eyes, she was sure he had also.

It was none of her business if Nick didn't want to stay in contact with his mother. But the thought bothered her. She knew he hadn't had a storybook childhood, but why ignore his mother? Faith would do anything to have just one more day with either one of her beloved parents.

*Don't get involved,* a little voice reminded her. *The*

*more distance between you and Nick Chandler, the better.*
Faith hoped she'd be able to heed her own warning.

She followed Nick into the backyard. Nick's expression immediately changed upon seeing the dog. "Hey, boy. Come here." Nick clapped his hands, bent down, and the beagle who'd been lying rather forlornly in the corner of the yard bounded into Nick's arms. "That's a boy!"

After minutes of patting, rubbing and mutual adoration, Nick turned to Faith, then the dog. "You know Faith, don't you?" he asked Legal.

Faith bent down and stroked the beagle's shiny coat. "Yeah, we've met a time or two."

Legal proceeded to lick Faith's cheek. He plastered his face to hers. She chuckled, but backed out of his way.

"Just like a woman. First they get you close, then they shove you away."

There was a note of teasing in his voice, but Faith had a feeling Nick believed those words with all his heart.

Mary walked out the back door and stood near Faith. "The dog likes you. I think my Nicky does too," she whispered low enough so Nick wouldn't hear. He was busy throwing a ball and the beagle was busy retrieving it.

"Oh, no, Mary. It's not like that. We've only just met. A few days ago. I—" She stopped because she realized that was a lie. She'd known Nick before, intimately.

"Ah, you have a boyfriend?"

"No, not exactly." She had Bill, but she wouldn't call him her boyfriend. They dated, enjoyed each other's company, had shared interests, but she hadn't felt anything remotely spectacular when he kissed her. And that had only happened a few times in the two months she'd gone out with him.

"Nicky's a good man."

"I'm sure he is."

"You'll come back sometime. Nicky will bring you."

"I, uh, thank you. Thank you for everything, the food, the company, everything. I'm glad we had this chance to get to know each other better."

"Yes. You're welcome here anytime. We're family now."

"Why yes. I suppose we are." It dawned on Faith that she and this warmhearted woman were indirectly related. "Hope is fortunate to have married into such a wonderful family. You know my parents died several years ago. I'm glad Hope has all of you."

Mary's smile was warm and gracious. "I love your sister. She makes my Tony very happy. But we are your family too. Don't forget that."

"Thank you," Faith said and put out her hand to say goodbye, just as Mary wrapped her arms around Faith, and gave her an enormous hug. Faith brought her arms around the affectionate woman and hugged back. "Goodbye, Mary. Don't worry about Legal. He'll have fun."

"I'm not worried about the dog." Mary glanced at Nick as he approached with Legal on a leash. "I know you'll take good care of him."

Nick kissed Mary again, thanking her. He ushered both Faith and the dog into his truck. The frisky canine sat between them. As Nick pulled away, Legal scooted onto Faith's lap to look out the window. She gave him a pat on the head. He looked at her with

round hopeful eyes. Faith was enamored. She patted
him again and stroked his soft ears. Satisfied, the dog
removed himself from Faith's lap to gain attention
from Nick.

Legal put his head on Nick's thigh and lay across
the seat. Nick scratched his ears. "I think we might
be creating a monster here. Pretty soon this dog's
going to have both of us wrapped around his . . .
paw."

Faith let out a low chuckle, watching man with dog.
"He is cute. I never had a pet growing up, but I always
wanted one."

"And why is that?"

"My father was adamant about not having pets.
The Chicago cop didn't want an animal wreaking
havoc in the house. He said my mother had enough
to do with both of us girls to raise. Of course Hope
sneaked a kitten into our room and we hid it for days.
She'd found this adorable long-haired gray with huge
blue eyes and couldn't let it go. I think my mother
knew, but never said a word. And you know what, I
think Dad knew too. He was a softie at heart. He must
have figured if he pretended not to know, then he
didn't have to enforce his rule."

"Sounds like he was okay."

"More than okay, he was a great dad. Stern, but
not unbendable."

Nick nodded. He asked, genuinely interested,
"What happened to the stray?"

"Oh, one day I found Hope crying in our room.
She'd found a lost kitten poster in our neighbor-
hood. The kitten belonged to a little girl. We both
took the kitten back. It was hard, but I convinced

Hope it was the right thing to do. My father taught us to do what's right. Always, without question."

"And you always do the right thing now?" He gave her a sideways glance.

"Yes, I do. Of course, Hope, well, she's different. She's always been the risk-taker in the family. I tend to walk the straight and narrow." Faith had envied that about her sister while growing up. Hope wasn't afraid to jump right into a new situation. She wasn't at all cautious. Maybe that's why she was a successful career woman with a loving new husband while Faith remained essentially alone.

Nick gave her a rueful look. Faith realized what he'd been thinking. She hadn't exactly been the picture of virtue that night in Palm Springs. "I bet you really believe that about yourself," he said bluntly.

"Of course I do. Listen, the one night we spent together doesn't make you an expert about me. Just as I don't know anything about you. We are strangers, Nick. It's best to remember that."

Nick grunted and kept his eyes on the road. Faith absently reached out to stroke the sleeping beagle next to her and touched Nick's strong, work-roughened hands. She felt the fine sprinkling of hair on his fingers before resting her hand next to his on Legal's back. They drove in silence the rest of the way home.

Nick's work area on the south side of the house received the greatest amount of the day's heat. And it was a scorcher today. Sweat ran down his face and soaked his white T-shirt as he hammered away at the wall unit he was building for the new room. His choice for a work space was probably not the wisest location, but it was closest to the room he was converting and he'd promised to stay out of Faith's way.

He pounded in another nail and thought about the annoying redhead. "Damn woman nearly got me arrested today," he muttered to the beagle resting under a shade tree. The dog's head lay comfortably on his front paws.

A shudder coursed the length of Nick's body, thinking about the rough way he'd been handled by the police. Being shoved up against the wall and handcuffed brought back many vivid memories. Of another time, another Nick. "It's been a long time, Legal."

For one brief moment this morning, he'd been that wayward snot-nosed kid caught shoplifting at Finley's market. The fear of being caught had mingled with the satisfaction of making his father come down to pick him up at the station. John Chandler had not been happy. But he'd had to sober up, shave and drive himself down to the market to retrieve Nick. It was almost worth the pounding Nick had gotten afterward. Hell, he'd been hungry, but he'd been hungry before and hadn't resorted to stealing.

As an adult, Nick understood his motives for stealing. It was his cry for help. His mother had abandoned him. His father spent his time passed out drunk in the filthy shanty they'd called home. Nick had to grow up fast in order to survive.

And today, thanks to one Faith McAllister, he'd been given a graphic reminder of the scared kid he'd been. The boy who was sneered at because his clothes were always dirty, the boy decent folks wouldn't allow their children near. And as a teen, the boy mothers warned their daughters about.

Thank God for Tony DiMartino and his family.

They'd made his life worth salvaging. He'd never forget them and their kindness.

Nick glanced at the shirt he'd flung onto a branch of a slender white birch tree and grimaced. The pristine white parchment envelope was nearly falling out of his shirt pocket. His mother's letter.

Another shudder coursed through his veins, but he would put that reminder out of his thoughts. For now.

Damn, he was having a hell of a day. As perspiration blanketed his back, he drew up the T-shirt, removing it along with his bad mood. "What the hell, I'm not going to get any more work done today. I need to cool off." He glanced at the lazy hound who had fallen asleep. "All right, I'll go it alone. You don't know what you're missing."

Nick wiped the sweat off his face with his bunched up T-shirt and headed for the house. As he strode through the living room, he caught a glimpse of movement out by the pool. He moved closer to the double-paned French doors to view a bikini-clad body soaking up the sun on an inflatable float. Faith looked peaceful as she rested on her stomach with her eyes closed.

Seeing her there, lying practically naked in that skimpy bikini, stirred his already heated body. He noted her creamy skin, long, incredibly soft legs, firm rounded breasts. He hadn't forgotten an inch of her.

He wanted her.

Hell, lust had nothing to do with any other emotion. He didn't have to like her, did he? He had no reason to be noble. Why couldn't he enjoy this time with her, then be the one to walk away? He had often daydreamed of doing that very thing.

Nick bounded up the stairs with renewed determination, trading work pants for cut-off jeans and at the last minute grabbed a clean towel from the linen closet. He was back outside within three minutes, staring at the floating goddess. She had no clue he was there.

"What the hell," he muttered. The woman had caused him enough grief for one day. He had just as much right to use the pool as she had. As the tiny rippling waves turned her float sideways, Nick noticed the straps to her bikini top were undone. She was probably in search of the ultimate tan. Then a wicked scheme entered his mind.

Nick studied the pool, wondering where would be the best place to dive in.

No, not dive. That wouldn't create enough of a splash.

He made a run for it, hoisted his body into midair and jumped in.

From underwater, he heard Faith scream.

# FIVE

Faith came out of the water sputtering. Nick watched her dip her hair back to remove it from her face. The brilliant sunlight cast a red-gold shine on her long mane, and water trickled down her face onto her shoulders as she stood up. Once she regained her composure, she scanned the pool until she saw him. Her eyes flashed green fire. "You did that on purpose!"

With arms folded, Nick lounged lazily against the far side watching her. As she glided through the pool coming out of the five-foot depth to the more shallow side, the view she offered him stole his breath. Her beautifully rounded breasts were caressed by water that had calmed since his jump.

It wasn't until she got close enough to see the look on his face—Nick couldn't keep the gleam of appreciation out of his expression—that she realized she had lost her bikini top. Nick clutched the small scrap of material in one hand.

"Oh!" Faith turned the shade of a flamingo. Adorably pink. She covered her breasts by crossing her hands over them and whirled around in the water.

Her wide-eyed startled expression, her sleek, wet body gleaming in the sunshine, her hands holding her generous bosom, nearly undid Nick. He moved through the water to reach her.

Clutching the tile for support with one arm, Faith threw her other arm out behind her. "Give that to me, Nick!" She wiggled her fingers.

Nick came up behind her, placing the black bikini top in her outstretched palm. "Calm down, Irish. It's nothing I haven't seen before," he whispered near her ear.

She gasped. "You're a dreadful man."

Nick chuckled. "I've been called worse."

She struggled to get her top back on. Her fingers trembled.

"Here, let me help."

"No! Go away."

Nick ignored her and took the black straps from behind, tying the one across her back first. Then he reached up, lifted her hair to one side and tied the one around her neck. Slowly, he let his fingers graze her soft skin.

"That really was an obnoxious thing to do," she reprimanded, once her top was secure.

"Small price to pay for nearly getting me arrested this morning, Faith."

Faith turned then. Nick had trapped her up against the tile of the pool. He wasn't backing off.

"I said I was sorry."

"I know." Nick searched her eyes. "Now, we're even."

She smiled.

"I just couldn't resist. I've wanted to play in the water with you since I first saw you in Palm Springs. I think you were wearing the same suit." Nick glanced down at the revealing bikini, and Faith blushed again.

"But I—I thought—"

He grinned. "You thought I'd never laid eyes on you before you walked into that bar."

She nodded.

"Honey, I'd spotted you long before that from the window in my hotel room." Nick moved to her side and braced his elbows up on the edge of the pool. He lifted his face to the sun. "You were hard to miss. The knock-out redhead in the black bikini."

"Really?" she asked softly.

"I watched men approach you. You were cool, aloof. I thought: rich bitch."

"I'm not like that."

Nick laughed. "Well, you're definitely not rich." She slugged him in the arm. "Ouch! Okay, I guess, you're not—"

"I'm not," she defended briskly.

"Still, it was quite a show. I spent the better part of the afternoon watching you. Your body was sending the right message, but as soon as the men approached, you lowered the ax. I counted five wounded."

Faith's hand shifted through the water as she spoke. "You make me sound so . . . calculating. I'm really not like that."

Nick put up his hands in surrender and kept his sarcasm to a minimum. "I know, you're really not like that."

She frowned. "What's the use? Believe what you want. I can't change your mind."

As far as Nick's mind went, she'd confused the hell out of him. He was sure she was a tease when he'd met her that evening in Palm Springs. She was out for one thing and one thing only, and he had been happy to oblige. He had witnessed her disintegrate a handful of men earlier in the day and frankly, his ego needed a jump-start. So when she'd sat down next to him on that barstool and flirted shamelessly, he had flirted back.

She'd been bold, sitting at the bar conversing with a low, sexy voice, wearing that little emerald green dress, hinting at pleasures to come. But once he'd gotten her up to his hotel room, she had changed to a timid, jittery, unsure woman. They sat and talked until two in the morning. Nick hadn't pushed. But when he'd realized how late it was, he'd stood and offered to walk her to her room. It was then that she had mustered her courage. She slid the straps of her dress down. "No, please, I really need to do this," she had said.

Nick had recognized fleeting anguish in her eyes, then desperation. He hadn't questioned her. He had needs of his own to take care of that night.

And when they made love, it had been like a blending of two souls. Incredible. It had never been better for Nick. He didn't understand the feeling then, he didn't now. Maybe that's why he'd been so angry when she'd run out the next day without a word.

"So what were you doing watching me from a hotel window?" she asked, interrupting his thoughts.

Nick drew in a deep breath. He turned to meet her eyes. "Drowning my sorrows with my smooth friend, Jack Daniels."

Faith was quiet for a while. She chewed on her lower lip. "What sorrows?"

Nick closed his eyes to the sun and let the warmth

seep into him. He didn't respond immediately. He knew Faith was waiting for his answer; he felt her eyes on him. He wasn't sure why he trusted her. He shouldn't. Maybe he liked the way she didn't rush to ask the question. She asked as if she knew it really wasn't any of her business. Her voice held a sincere tone. "I had agreed to meet my mother there. She never showed."

"Oh, I'm sorry."

"Don't be."

"Maybe she had a good reason, Nick. Did you ever hear from her again?"

A good reason to leave him holding the bag again? No, he didn't think so. She'd left him with a worthless drunk of a father when Nick was twelve years old. It hadn't been an easy thing to do, agreeing to see her after almost twenty years. He had, in a sense, written her off for good. But he'd opened his heart, only to have it broken again that day in Palm Springs.

The same day he'd met Faith.

Nick scooped up a handful of water and splashed his face. The liquid refreshed him, renewed him. "She sent a letter to Mrs. D for me six months ago. I ripped it up."

Faith's eyes were soft when she took his arm. "I can't begin to understand what you've been through, but I know you have another letter from your mother now. Why not find out what she has to say?"

He was standing in a pool with a barely clad gorgeous woman. Her hands were on him, her eyes soft and sweet and he was talking about his mother. Was he crazy? He glanced down at Faith. "That's not what I want to do right now."

"What do you want to do?" Her question was innocent. Nick had nothing innocent planned. He plastered his body against hers and stared at her lips. "I want to kiss you senseless, Irish."

When she gazed up into his eyes, he saw the softness evaporate, replaced by a develish twinkle. "Oh yeah?"

He liked putting that look on her face. "Yeah." He brought his head down inches from hers. She moved briskly, ducking under his arm and scooped up water with both hands, splashing him all over.

She swam away laughing. "And I thought you wanted to play in the pool!"

Nick swam after her, splashing as he went. "I can play with the best of them, Faith. You haven't got a chance."

Nick reached her quickly and dunked her. She came up shrieking, then dodged him again. When he caught up to her, she cried, "No, no, no!." He loosened his grip. With a deep thrust, she sent water flying into his face and raced off again.

It took him a second to catch his breath. She wasn't easy prey. He'd always known that. He took off after her and grabbed her arms in mid-air before she could splash him again. Her face beamed with joy, until she glanced at her right arm. Then all the color drained from her face. She looked panicked. "Oh no! My bracelet! Nick, it's gone. I've lost my charm bracelet."

He might have thought this was another ploy to get away from him, but her expression was too bleak. Even a seasoned actress couldn't have put on such a show. "Okay, don't panic. We'll find it. Were you wearing it when you were on the float?"

"I don't remember. But I never take it off! Maybe it came loose when you jumped in and I went under."

Nick scanned the bottom of the pool looking for something shiny. He didn't see anything resembling her bracelet. "Just wait here." He dove in and swam the distance of the pool and back, searching. He came up out of the water to find Faith's gaze on him, her expression hopeful. Nick shook his head and met her on the steps of the pool.

"You didn't see it?" Moisture began to well up in her eyes.

"I'm sorry. I'll keep look—" Nick spotted Legal sauntering by with something dangling from his mouth. Nick grinned, hoping he wasn't wrong. "Come here, boy."

Legal had no qualms about bounding into the water. He landed with an ungraceful spatter. The dog started splashing toward the steps, keeping his head above water, the shiny object between his teeth. He swam fast, only stopping once he'd reached them. "Whoa! I didn't mean for you to jump in. Let's see what you have."

"Nick," Faith cried with a note of relief, "it's my bracelet."

Nick pried the bracelet from Legal's mouth and glanced at it before handing it over to Faith. "Looks okay. No damage done."

"Oh, thank goodness!" Faith held the thin strip of gold as if it were set with a hundred one-carat diamonds. She checked it over cautiously. Once she appeared satisfied, she sat down on the edge of the pool and put the dog on her lap. "Oh, you're a sweet little Legal Beagle, aren't you." She kissed his head and rubbed his stomach, and the dog licked her face. "Did you find my bracelet in the bushes over there?"

The dog panted happily in reply.

Nick put his hands on his hips. "I nearly drowned looking for that bracelet. What's my reward?"

Faith chuckled and set the dog away from her. She held out her wrist. "You get to put it back on. The clasp's a bit tricky. I'm surprised it even came off."

Nick sat down next to her. "Something's wrong with this picture; I spend all my time *dressing* you."

She turned serious eyes on him. "Thank you, Nick. I appreciate your help trying to find it."

Nick undid the clasp and placed it around her wrist, then secured the bracelet. "How'd it come off anyway? It's a tight fit. Doesn't look like it could slide off and the clasp was still closed."

Faith smiled, looking down at her wrist. "Maybe it's magic."

Nick began fingering each clover. "Interesting design." When he touched the second one, he could swear it was nearly warm enough to burn. Perhaps it had been lying in the sun.

"What's wrong?" Faith asked, noticing his puzzled expression.

"Nothing," Nick answered, staring at the charms. "It looks old."

Faith nodded. "It's a family heirloom. Hope gave it to me the night before her wedding. Every female member of our family has worn it sometime in their life."

"So that's why you panicked. It's an important part of your family's heritage. I'm glad we found it."

"Me too." Faith shivered, realizing the entire backyard was suddenly enveloped in shade. "The sun's almost down."

Nick brought her a towel and watched as she wrapped herself up. He was feeling a slight chill himself. The thought of warm clothes and relaxing with Faith this evening sounded pretty good. "Maybe we should go in and get dry. How about I pick up Chinese food for dinner?"

Faith hesitated. "I'd like that, but I can't. I have a date."

The words slashed through him. But why should he give a damn? He had no claim on her, although he'd thought all this afternoon about kissing her again, feeling her in his arms.

He shrugged as he grabbed a towel and headed for the house. "No problem."


Faith studied Nick from the doorway while he was working up on a ladder, measuring, marking, concentrating on the construction of the new room. His jeans hung low on his waist. From the back, she noted his strong build, powerful muscles and tanned skin. Nick was in the habit of not wearing a shirt. Faith wanted to believe she was unaffected seeing him that way, but in truth, she hadn't really gotten used to seeing him unclothed. Her breath caught in her throat and she had to force words out in order to speak whenever he was around, wearing next to nothing, oozing his own brand of male sensuality.

Although those times had been few. She hadn't seen too much of him in the last two days since their playful banter by the pool.

She thought he was avoiding her, and that was precisely what she wanted. She went about the business of vacationing, he the business of room conversion. Although she'd heard him throughout the house, he never attempted to approach her. Whenever they bumped into each other, he'd been polite and smiled then went about whatever he'd been doing.

It was driving Faith crazy!

Faith cleared her throat not too daintily. Nick turned around on the ladder. "Hi, roommate, what's up?"

Faith stepped into the room. Ignoring the work he was doing, she directed her full attention on him. "I found your shirt by the pool and threw it in with my wash. I'm just returning it." She laid the folded shirt down on the desktop.

Nick stepped off the ladder. "Thank you."

"I also found your mother's letter. It must have dropped out of the pocket," she said slowly, meeting his dark gaze. He reached his hand out and took the envelope.

"Okay," he said, then stuffed the envelope into his shirt pocket again.

"Aren't you going to open it?"

He shrugged with nonchalance, but a flicker of anguish flashed in his eyes. "I haven't decided."

"Maybe your mother had good reason—"

"Don't lecture me, Faith, and don't defend her. I said I haven't decided. Let it drop."

There was an edge to his voice that wouldn't allow an argument.

"Are you going out?" he asked abruptly. His eyes scanned her attire from her simple high-collared white lace dress down to her very proper slingback pumps.

"What? Oh, yes. Sorry for the intrusion. I'll just let you get back to work."

When Nick picked up a screwdriver and resumed his work Faith turned to leave, but his husky voice blared across the room, startling her. "You're fooling yourself, Irish."

Faith whirled around. "I beg your pardon."

He pointed the screwdriver at her and gestured. "You, in that get-up. That's not you."

Faith let out a wry laugh. "And what makes you such an expert?"

He arched both brows and gave her a slow smile.

Faith would never live down that one fateful night, not with Nick taunting her at every turn. Anger bubbled within her. She tried to tamp it down, but it insisted on surfacing. She steeled her voice, making each word count. "Oh no, Nick Chandler, don't you dare go there. You don't know me, you only think you do. One night is all we had, all there will ever be."

"Christ, you look like a church mouse in that outfit, and you've got your hair twisted in a tight 'don't-touch-me' knot."

"Nick!"

"What happened to the woman I met in Palm Springs, Irish? The one who knocked my socks off?"

"Damn it, Nick. I *invented* her! Heather O'Leary was the name of a personality I invented for that one night because I was too afraid to be myself. I'm more at home with a good book. I'm not exciting—"

"Like hell you're not! Lady, you turned me inside out that night."

Faith cringed at Nick's curt assessment of their

night together. "I'm sorry, Nick. I truly am. I didn't mean to deceive you."

"Then why did you run away from me that morning, Faith? When you admit that to yourself, it will be a start."

"I don't want to *start* anything. It's over. Finished."

Nick moved in closer. His strong jaw set stubbornly and his dark gaze honed in on her, seething with restrained anger. "You still haven't told me why."

Faith drew in a deep, soulful breath. She had no pride left when it came to Nick. "Because my devoted fiancé Peter ran off with a blonde bimbo, that's why!" Faith held back her tears. Even though she'd gotten over losing Peter, the sting of betrayal and the humiliation that followed had hurt her deeply.

Nick leaned on his workbench with folded arms, studying her with cold disdain. Faith couldn't tear her eyes away from his penetrating stare, nor could she stop the single tear from rolling down her cheek. Nick blinked several times as his anger faded. Then, slowly, he reached for her. "Come here," he coaxed with a soft tone that surprised her. He turned her around and drew her into the circle of his arms, setting her back against his chest. She went willingly, gliding into his comfort. "Go on," he coaxed. "Tell me."

Faith continued, feeling relief at finally being able to explain to Nick about her deception. She began quietly, "The blonde bimbo had more body piercings than all of the fans at a Metallica concert put together. She was so utterly and completely different than me. I was crushed by Peter's betrayal, and I think that I was just as crushed because I couldn't see the signs. I felt like a fool, and I didn't like feeling that way."

"So then you got mad," Nick responded.

She nodded. "Peter not only left me, but his teaching job as well. He planned on opening a body piercing shop with her. I just hope she puts a few holes in him. Where it counts."

Nick chuckled in her ear. "Sorry. But I think it's a good thing you got rid of the guy."

"He dumped *me*. But, I believe now, it was for the best. I didn't really know him, did I?"

"No, guess not. So, then what?"

"Well, I packed my bags and headed for Palm Springs. I needed to make a break with the past. I needed . . . certain reassurances."

"You needed to feel desirable again?"

"My ego had taken too much punishment," she admitted on a soft breath, hardly believing she could be so direct and honest with Nick. "But I've never been so impetuous, so wild, so . . . stupid, in my life."

"Hey! I take offense."

"No, not about you. That part was wonderful. But it shouldn't have happened. I shouldn't have let anything happen between us."

He stroked her arms tenderly, up and down, making her shiver with pleasure. "Tell me again how wonderful it was."

Faith blushed, clear down to her toes. It was a good thing she had her back to Nick so he couldn't see her turn the color of ripe tomatoes. And she felt less inhibited this way, without their eyes meeting. "Well," she said wistfully, "you saved me somehow. I went back home renewed. You helped restore my femininity, if that makes any sense. Could you tell I wasn't very experienced?"

She heard Nick swallow. "No. You handled yourself quite well." His arms about her tightened. "I had trouble forgetting you."

Faith closed her eyes. She felt herself softening to him. She hadn't forgotten him either. There were so many things she wanted to say. "But you did."

He didn't answer. After a long moment of silence, he said, "I searched for you, I had a friend of mine spend a couple of days trying to find out anything he could about Heather O'Leary."

She let out a low, pained sigh.

"Of course, he came up empty."

Faith wanted to dig a hole and crawl into it. "Why did you want to find me?"

Nick's wry laugh was self-deprecating. "No matter what you think about me, I'm responsible when it comes to the opposite sex. I had to find out if you were okay."

"You mean pregnant?"

"Yeah."

"We used protection, Nick, as I recall—"

In a brisk move, Nick set her away from him. "Ah, hell, I'm not your big brother, Faith. Listen, I'm glad you got it off your chest. I'm glad I was of service to you in Palm Springs. But I still think you're fooling yourself."

Faith missed his comforting arms. And his jibe about being of service to her hurt. She had been trying to thank him. "Why do you think I'm fooling myself?"

Nick scratched his head and looked her over. "I

think you really are that passionate woman I met in Palm Springs, but you just don't want to admit it."

Faith's pulse accelerated as his words sunk in. A shiver ran up and down her spine. "No, I don't think so."

"You talked endlessly about your design business. Now I know you don't have one, but I bet you'd love to. And I also think you'd be good at it, but you're afraid to try."

Panic gripped her. He was hitting close to home. "How can you know all that?"

"Because you were so enthusiastic about it. Maybe you invented all that, but your ideas, your plans were real to you way before you met me in that bar."

Faith stared at him without blinking. Could what he said be true? Was she really the bold, creative woman she'd wanted to be for him?

"You pretended to be someone you're not, but maybe that's who you really want to be," Nick continued, determined to win his point.

"No, I—" Faith rubbed her forehead. He was confusing her. "I'm getting a headache."

Nick gave her a sly grin. "Maybe you should cancel your date. Geez, Faith, I caught a glimpse of the guy the other night. How old is he, fifty, fifty-five?"

"Why—you!" Faith stomped her foot down. "He's not that old. I'll have you know he's a very nice man. And what's wrong with me dating an older man, anyway?"

Nick took a step closer. "So then, it's serious?"

Faith closed her eyes momentarily. "No. I didn't say that. I . . . like him, that's all. We're friends."

She knew she'd never have stronger feelings for Bill than what she felt right now. Faith cared about the man, admired him and enjoyed his company, but nothing more would ever come of it. In truth, she had begun seeing him to get Hope to stop trying to set her up on blind dates. And her scheme had worked. Until now. Hope and Tony were probably having a good laugh somewhere right now, thinking how they had set her up on the longest blind date of all. A two-week blind date with Nick.

Faith still wasn't entirely sure they had deliberately set out to trick her, but knowing her sister . . .

"Faith?"

"Huh?"

Nick smirked. "I think I hear your *friend* knocking on the front door."

Faith stiffened. She didn't really want to go out with Bill tonight. She'd called him because Nick had been ignoring her. Now that she and Nick were talking, communicating, she found that she liked being with him. Arrogant, overly confident, audacious, Nick Chandler was still more entertaining than most of the men Faith had known. Damn him anyway. "Yes, well, I'd better go. Don't work too hard tonight," she said on her way out the door.

"Don't plan to. I have a date tonight too."

Faith's heart slammed in her chest as she moved to the front door. Her head throbbed even more as she realized she would spend the entire evening wondering who Nick was dating.

And wondering why she cared so much.


Nick pulled his truck around back, slamming the door as he got out. He was glad his date with Debra was over. It had been a mistake. He'd danced with her at Tony's wedding and the persistent woman had insisted on having him over for dinner. He'd only accepted because at the time, he was still furious with Faith.

Debra served him a delicious meal. The woman could cook, he admitted.

Only, Nick had the feeling he was meant to be the dessert.

He had needed a distraction from Faith, but all night long, Faith's admission and her apology for deceiving him when they'd first met came popping into his mind. And the way she felt when he'd held her in his arms this evening put Debra far out of his thoughts.

Faith could heat his blood faster than a raging fire. He had set her away from him earlier that evening, or she would have detected the full extent of her appeal to him. His body had reacted to her. It didn't matter that Faith looked as if she'd been dressed for Sunday school, he knew the woman underneath. Her innocent and sweet look made her all the more tempting.

Nick warned himself to steer clear. Faith didn't know her own mind, and Nick had been through enough bad experiences with women who hadn't known what they were all about. He wasn't going down that road again. Ever.

He entered the kitchen through the back door. Faith sat at the table in the dimly lit room, sipping a cup of fresh coffee. Nick flung his keys on the counter and opened the refrigerator. "You're home early."

Faith glanced his way. "So are you."

"Yeah, well, I didn't stay for dessert." Nick pulled

out the last piece of apple pie Mrs. D had sent over the other day. "Want to share?"

"No, thanks. I know you can polish that off all by yourself. Want some coffee?" Faith started to rise.

"Sure, but you sit. I'll get it."

Nick poured himself a cup and sat down at the table. "How was your evening?"

"Nice. We went to CityWalk at Universal Studios and had dinner at Wolfgang Puck's. Have you been up there yet?"

Nick shook his head. "No. I've been out of town a lot. Spent most of last year in a resort town near Bass Lake, building vacation cottages."

Faith sipped her coffee and nodded. "Do you have any roots at all, Nick?"

He let out a small chuckle before taking a bite of pie. "Sure I do. I have a place I'm building for myself between jobs. Right now, it's more than half finished."

"So where do you live? Do you always bunk with Tony when you're in town?"

He shook his head while sipping from his mug. "No. There's a trailer set up on my property. It's clean, has all the necessary comforts. When I'm in town, it's home."

"So why were you so stubborn about staying here? Did you do it just to drive me crazy?"

Nick laughed. He had to. The woman was more perceptive than she seemed. He *had* wanted to make her life miserable. "Well, that was one reason," he said with honesty.

Faith looked away. "I guess I deserved that."

"But the real reason is that my place is about an hour from here. I didn't want to waste my time driving. I knew I'd be putting in long hours to get the room done on time."

"Is that why you're home so early?"

"I'm dedicated, but not that dedicated. If I'd wanted to stay longer, I would have." If he'd been with a woman he wanted, nothing would have stopped him. If he'd been on a date with Faith—

She looked into his eyes. He saw the questions there. She was dying of curiosity. "Debra is a fine cook."

Faith put her cup down quickly, sloshing coffee over her hand. She didn't flinch. Nick assumed she wasn't burned, at least, not by the coffee. "Debra? Debra Conklin? You went out with her?"

Nick shrugged, enjoying her discomfort. "She invited me to dinner."

Faith's eyes widened and her face paled. She couldn't mask the look on her face, though Nick thought she tried. Jealousy. Plain, simple, green-eyed jealousy. Nick didn't know if that was a good thing or not. He wanted to revel in it anyway.

"And?" she asked indignantly.

Nick scraped the chair back and stood up, taking his plate and cup to the sink. "And nothing. She's not my type."

Silence.

Nick turned to her. "What? You don't have a comment."

"I—no. I don't, as a matter of fact."

"Good, because I don't pry into your affairs."

That got her dander up. "I don't have affairs, Nick. Besides, I won't be seeing much of Bill anymore. He's moving to Oakland."

"What's in Oakland?"

"He's got a son going to college at Berkeley, and a job offer there. I'm happy for him."

"And what about you?"

"I'm fine. I told you we were just friends."

Nick didn't want to think about the commotion rumbling around inside of him or the elation he felt. Instead, he thought of business. He stood over her with hands on hips. "Listen, I don't know what you've got planned for tomorrow, but I'm at a dead halt with the room. I think you could help me, if you had the time."

"Me? What could I do?"

"Tony gave me free rein with the room, but I'm afraid I don't know your sister well enough to know her tastes. I've picked out some samples for wallpaper, fabric for the window coverings and the window seat I designed. I could use your input. You'd not only be doing me a favor, but Hope as well. I'm not too sure about what I have in mind."

Faith's face lit up. Nick could just about see her imagination working already. "Yes, I think I'd love to help. What time?"

"Meet me downstairs after breakfast."

"Is nine okay? I want to get in my run first."

"I hear you getting up early every morning. How long have you been jogging?"

Faith smiled. "Only since forever. You should try it sometime. It's great exercise. Clears the mind."

"Don't mind if I do. What time do we start tomorrow?"

Faith stood. She had a look of shock on her face as she clutched the top of the kitchen chair. "We? Nick, I don't know. I run six, sometimes seven miles. If you're not used to—"

"Don't worry about me. If I don't keep up, you can leave me in the dust. What time?"

"Seven."

"I'll be ready."

Nick's mood had definitely picked up. He was going to spend the day with Faith. No longer dating, she was more available to him than she had ever been. He recognized the emotion that had washed over him after she had made her admission earlier: pure relief. Climbing the stairs, he pursed his lips and whistled a loud tune to block out the warnings that sounded in his head.

Warnings he managed quite successfully to ignore.

# SIX

Nick waited for Faith by the front door. Wearing his jogging shorts and a beat up old UCLA Bruins T-shirt with the sleeves cut off, he did a series of stretching exercises. He began with long body moves, lifting arms up and pulling, then bending at the waist for a good leg stretch. Next he worked on the calf muscles. He did a couple of minutes worth of squats, laughing when his rusty joints complained. "You're not as young as you used to be," he muttered.

Faith came up from behind, smirking. "How old are you, Nick?"

Nick bounced up on his Nike Air running shoes. "Thirty-two." He ran in place. "Want to warm up?"

"I'm warmed up and ready to go."

She sure was. Nick noted her jogging clothes with a silent groan. She wore light gray, very short shorts and a white skintight sports top that crisscrossed in the back. Four beautiful inches of smooth skin separated the two garments. Instead of a severe bun, she wore her hair in a loose ponytail at the top of her head.

She certainly didn't look matronly today. No, today she looked every bit the all-American beauty, California style.

Nick followed Faith out the front door. She started jogging at a slow pace. "I usually run through the streets until I reach Pacific Coast Highway, then I make a right and head to the beach."

"Sounds fine to me. It's your run. I'm just tagging along."

Nick let Faith take the lead. After a short while she turned her head. "You okay back there?"

"Just dandy. I like the view." She didn't see his grin. There was nothing quite like viewing a sexy woman jogging. All legs, sleek and tanned, leading to twin cheeks that peeked out from skimpy shorts. Nick found even the bounce of her ponytail appealing.

"Did you go to UCLA?" she called out.

Nick caught up to her as they rounded a curve in the road. They were on the coast highway now, heading toward Zuma Beach. "Nah, this shirt must have been one of Tony's throwaways. I went to the community college."

They jogged for a time without speaking. It was a comfortable silence. Nick didn't feel like he had to make conversation with her. At some point, they'd reached an amiable standoff in their relationship.

Nick scoffed at his own musings. What exactly was their relationship? He didn't know, but planned on spending the next few days finding out.

They jogged to the first lifeguard station at Zuma Beach. "Want to get a drink? There's a water fountain by the restrooms."

"Sure thing."

Nick took his cue from Faith when she stopped by the snack area. "This is the halfway point. How are you holding up?"

Nick grinned. "How do I look?"

Faith studied him for a few seconds. With a note of surprise, she said, "You're not even sweating."

"But you are," he said, teasing. He pointed to her top that was nearly transparent from perspiration. Two well-defined, pert nipples were evident. Nick thought it a beautiful sight.

"How very like you to point that out, Nick."

Nick chuckled, glad she teased him back. They took turns at the water fountain, then resumed their jog.

Once they reached the street close to Tony's house, Nick wound his arm around Faith's waist, slowing her.

"What's wrong" she asked, almost pulling to a dead stop.

"Nothing." He grinned again. "Want to race home?"

Faith pouted. She looked adorable when she made that little girl face. "That's not a good idea. We should slow down, not speed up at the end."

"Chicken?"

"What?" She smiled and her eyes twinkled.

"You heard me." Nick egged her on. "Afraid you can't beat me? You're the seasoned jogger. I'm the lowly straggler."

Her chin tilted up and her green eyes flashed with determination. "I can beat you any time, any place, any *way*, Nick Chandler."

"I'll give you a head start."

"No way. We do this together, on equal terms, or all bets are off."

Nick shrugged. "Fine with me. From this point to the front door. Ready . . . set . . . go!"

Faith took off like a shot. He had to give her credit,

she was fast. Nick let her get halfway home before he poured it on. He came up next to her and yanked on her ponytail. She screamed and slapped at his hand. They stayed neck and neck until Nick sprinted the last twenty yards to the house, leaving Faith pretty much in the dust. He gave the front door a sharp smack, then threw himself onto the grass, out of breath.

Faith fell onto the lawn next to him. Her bountiful chest heaved up and down. Nick allowed his eyes to linger a moment, then on a deep sigh, he turned to stare up at the low-lying gray clouds.

"Let me guess, you were on the track team."

Nick chuckled. "City champs, two years in a row."

"Sprinter?"

"Yep."

"You tricked me."

"Yep. But you enjoyed it. Admit it, Faith. You had fun."

"I refuse to admit anything." Faith folded her arms across her chest, but there was laughter in her voice. And when he turned to look at her, a wide grin brightened her face.

"Admit it."

"No way."

Nick brought his finger up to tickle her ribs. Hell, he had to touch her somewhere. She was driving him crazy. She squirmed, trying to get his hand away, all the while giggling. "Stop it, Nick. Stop!"

"Admit it."

"No."

Thank goodness, she was so stubborn. It gave him a legitimate reason to keep his hands on her, which he did. Both hands were busy tickling, finding sensitive spots on her body, gliding across her bare skin. She shoved and pushed at him, but Nick wouldn't let up. His body tumbled onto hers. Tears of laughter streamed down her face. Nick brought his face close and stared into her eyes, stilling his hands once they'd settled just under her breasts.

Faith's big green eyes widened in response. "I like seeing you laugh." Nick took in her rosy cheeks and red lips. She was flushed with color from the jog, from the race, from his tickling. "You look incredibly beautiful right now."

"I'm hot and sweaty and—"

"Say thank you, Irish." But Nick didn't give her the chance. He kissed her full on the lips, letting his mouth become familiar again with her taste. He wanted to go on kissing her forever, but he knew he had to stop. They were on Tony's front lawn. He'd almost been arrested on this lawn. Discretion was in order. He wouldn't embarrass Tony and Hope. He sat up, bracing his elbows on his knees.

Slowly, Faith sat up too. She was quiet, and he caught her softly touching her lips. Staring at the stubby palm tree straight ahead, he asked, "Do you still want to help me this morning?"

"Yes," she said in a whisper.

Nick stood up, reaching out his hand. She took it and he helped her up. Faith brought her eyes to his. "Nick?"

"Hmmm?"

"I did have fun."

Faith showered quickly, then hurried down to the kitchen for a bowl of Grape Nuts. Legal was at her heels. The beagle followed her everywhere, often looking at her with big toffee-colored eyes that spoke of intense loyalty. Faith was smitten.

She spoiled the dog rotten. Reaching down, she stroked his head and slipped him a piece of buttered toast. He licked all the butter off before gobbling up the bread. "Good boy."

"Good boy, nothing." Nick stood in the doorway, smelling fresh and clean, wearing a pair of jeans and a chambray work shirt.

"He is a good dog, Nick." Faith smiled and stroked the beagle's shiny coat with a long, exaggerated motion.

"That dog's a traitor. He was my best friend until you showed up."

"Um, such a pity. Shows he has good taste."

"And does he sleep right next to your bed at night?"

"Heavens, no. He sleeps *on* the bed." Faith drank the last of her orange juice.

Nick took a long, leisurely look at her body, eyeing her with blatant interest. His hot expression stirred her blood, making her want things she shouldn't. "Never said the dog was stupid. Just a traitor."

Faith covered up her surprised reaction by laughing, then piled her dishes in the sink. "I'll meet you downstairs in a minute. I just want to go up and finish drying this soggy mop." Faith always had to air dry her hair before she could do much with it.

"Leave it that way, Faith."

"Damp and curly?"

Nick put his hands in his back pockets and took a step closer. His gaze traveled over her hair, then he lifted his dark penetrating eyes to her. "Yeah."

"Okay, if you're in that much of a rush." Faith

whizzed by him and headed toward the small staircase leading to the lower level.

"I'm in no rush at all. I like your hair down."

Faith bounded down the five steps. She called up to him, "Oh, I thought you were converting a room." She heard Nick's laughter as he followed her down the steps.

Once inside the new home office, Nick showed Faith his decorating ideas. Faith was glad he had called her in to help. Although he had sound judgment, Faith knew her sister better than anyone. While Hope was efficient in business, and liked to keep order, there was also a whimsical side to her that should be brought out in the room.

"No drapes. Hope hates drapes. I'd have to see samples, of course, but I think painted wood shutters would be best. We can try a light color, maybe ivory. It's easier to adjust the light filtering in with wide shutters. And since one window faces the ocean, she could have an unobstructed view."

Next she went over the carpet samples, picking out a creamy beige thick pile that would blend nicely with the color of paint she had in mind. Faith fingered through the cardboard strips of paint samples, finding a soft misty green that was perfect. "Nick, my sister only likes wallpaper when it doesn't look like wallpaper. Why bother with papering the walls, when I know she'd love this? This color is soft, and it's one of Hope's favorites. And if you paint the crown molding the same color as the shutters, it would tie the room together."

Standing close, Nick put his head down, listening intently to her ideas. With an easy nod, he agreed. "Okay, sounds good," he said without question.

"What about the wood? I had a medium walnut stain in mind."

Faith took in the room as a whole. Nick's work was impeccable. He had a penchant for fine detail. There were many special touches about the room that spoke of his talent and the love he had for his work.

Faith glanced with a lopsided smile at the his-and-hers computer desks standing side by side. There were tall oak bookcases, beautifully constructed and shelving that took up more than half of the room. "Nick, again, I'd have to see some samples, but I think with the amount of wood in here, you'd have to go lighter. Maybe whitewash the oak. Hope likes an open, airy look. What do you think Tony would say?"

"Right about now, Tony would give his wife the Taj Mahal. The man's got it bad."

Faith chuckled. "You're probably right. But Tony has to work in here too."

"He won't mind. If Hope is happy, then he'll be happy. That's the kind of person he is."

Faith sighed. She knew he was right, and the unconditional pride in Nick's tone told her how much Tony's friendship meant to him.

"What about fabric for the window seat?" Nick asked, looking at a bench that fit along the angular three-sided window he'd installed.

An idea popped into Faith's head as she mentally measured the bench seat. Excitement coursed through her veins, but she didn't want to voice her thoughts just yet; this was Nick's gift to both Tony and Hope. She didn't want to intrude.

"Faith, what is it?"

"Oh, nothing."

Nick gave her a knowing smile. "There's something bouncing around in that brain of yours. Out with it."

"I just thought—well, it's your gift to them and all. I wouldn't want to impose, but I'd love to—"

"I can use all the help I can get with decorating. It's not exactly my strong point. What would you love to do?"

"I'd love to make up the bench seat for them. I've got a fabric in mind I know Hope would love, and I can upholster the seat, make a few pillows. And I could find a matching fabric for their chair seats and do them too." She lifted her eyes to meet his smiling ones. "How would you feel about that?"

He blew out a breath. "You'd be doing me a big favor."

"I'd love to do it." Satisfied, Faith took another quick glance around the room, imagining the way the new DiMartino office would look when it was finished. "This is going to be a wonderful surprise for my sister."

Nick agreed. Shortly after, they drove to the Home Club, a design emporium featuring everything from bathroom fixtures to exquisite window treatments. With a quick eye for what she needed, Faith made her selections for the wood shutters, as well as the paint and stain needed to complete the work.

Nick approved them without a qualm, which bolstered her confidence. She knew what she was doing, but somewhere along the line, it was important to her that Nick also be satisfied. He placed a great deal of trust in her ability. She didn't want to let him down.

As a way of thanking her, Nick took Faith out to

an early dinner. They dined at a casual seaside restaurant that boasted the best Hawaiian fare in the area.

After dinner, they drove along the Pacific Coast Highway, enjoying the distant sounds of roaring waves and a starry night sky. Faith leaned her head back against the seat and relished a sensation of inner peace. She was having a wonderful vacation. She turned her head to take a peek at the man behind the steering wheel. Handsome, even in his casual work clothes, Faith wondered how much of her enjoyment of her vacation could be attributed to being with Nick Chandler.

She feared the answer. Nick was not the man for her. He still believed she wasn't the woman she claimed to be. Yet, in her heart, Faith knew him to be wrong. He wanted the sexy, tempting vixen, the confident woman that Faith had invented for one day, one year ago. He couldn't accept her as the real Faith McAllister. He probably didn't even like her. But when he kissed her, for one fleeting moment, she wished she could be the woman Nick wanted.

When they pulled up in the driveway, Faith turned to him. "Thanks, Nick. I can't remember having a better meal. I'm stuffed. Couldn't eat another bite."

"That's too bad, because for the last few miles, I've been thinking of two giant-sized scoops of Starbuck's Mocha Java ice cream. I hear it calling to me."

Faith got out of the car and faced him over the hood. "You bought that yesterday. It's almost all gone."

Nick rested his arms on the car door and smiled. "Guilty as charged. I know there are at least three scoops left, though. Want one?"

Faith thought about experimenting with a new ice cream flavor. "Mocha Java, huh?"

"With swirls of chocolate."

"I don't know." She pressed her hand to her stomach. "I'm so full."

"I won't guarantee there'll be any left by tomorrow," he said earnestly.

"Keep talking." Faith walked around the front of the car, meeting him halfway. "You're tempting me." And not just with ice cream, Faith thought ruefully.

"Last chance, Faith." Nick put out his hand, his eyes alight in boyish amusement. There was no way she could refuse.

Just as Faith lifted her hand to his, a slight pain nipped at her wrist. She glanced down at her bracelet to find that although the charms on either side lay flat, the second gold clover stood on end, balancing itself on its fine thin edge. And then just as quickly, the charm which had defied gravity for a prolonged moment in time, was mysteriously back in place.

Warily, Faith looked at Nick, who hadn't appeared to notice anything out of the ordinary.

"Well?" Wearing a charming smile, he stood waiting, with one hand reaching for hers.

A bit shaken by the odd occurrence, she dared one more glance at her bracelet, noting nothing unusual. The Triple Charm looked like an ordinary charm bracelet. She put her hand in his. "And you thought I wasn't a risk-taker," she ventured bravely.

But even as they laughed, a haunting shiver ran down her spine.

# SEVEN

Later, returning from a long walk with Legal, Nick removed the dog's leash, patted him on the head, then bounded up the stairs. Legal's insistent barking and whimpering had Nick turning around on the staircase and heading back downstairs. One look at the dog, scraping his paws against the glass on the French door leading to the backyard, told Nick the lovestruck canine had found Faith. Nick peered out the glass too, muttering to his canine friend, "Can't say that I blame you, boy. Okay, out you go."

Nick let the dog out, then stepped outside himself. Faith was sipping wine from a large goblet while she soaked luxuriously in the hot tub. Legal reached her first and sat on the terracotta tiles right by Faith's head. "Hello, sweet little beagle," she cooed. To Nick, she lifted her wineglass and asked, "Care to join me?"

Nick put his hands in the back pockets of his jeans and strolled over. "For a drink or a dip?"

She eyed him over the goblet as she gulped a large sip. "Both."

Nick raised his brows. "If that's an invitation, you don't have to ask twice."

She giggled. "The water's great, Nicky."

"I'll be right in." Nick dashed up to his bedroom, discarded his jeans and pulled on a pair of swim trunks. Minutes later, he was back down by the hot tub and in the water. He sunk into the steamy depths, hot liquid bubbling around him. "Mmmm. It does feel great."

He sat directly across from Faith. She was wearing the black bikini again, and her lustrous hair was down, flowing in waves around her face and shoulders. "Good idea. Even better than ice cream."

She fingered the rim of her glass. "Glad you like it."

Nick nodded as Faith poured herself another tall glass of wine. "Want some?"

"Not right now."

"You know something, Nick?" she began, then hiccupped.

She didn't look his way, but instead studied the wine goblet as if it held the secrets of the universe. "Did you know that Faith Heather McAllister has never once in her life gotten drunk out of her mind?"

Nick eyed the bottle of Chardonnay sitting on the small table beside the spa. Most of the wine was gone. "You're on your way now," he said, finally realizing her intent this evening.

She giggled and poured another swallow down her throat. She looked at Nick seductively, with half-closed eyes. "Come sit closer, Nicky."

Nick blew out a deep breath. The woman was tempting. With the faint glow of moonlight illuminating her lovely face and droplets of water glistening on her creamy skin, Nick had a mind to do much more than merely sit closer.

When she hiccupped, giggled, hiccupped again, then brought her lips to the wineglass, Nick rose out of the water. "Okay, that's it." He was up the steps and out of the spa, reaching for the bottle of wine. Splashing water as he went, he walked to the edge of the garden and emptied what was left in the bottle under an azalea bush.

"Hey, Nick, you're no fun. I'm"—she hiccupped again—"getting drunk."

Nick put his hands on his hips and looked down at her. "I lived with a drunk all my young life. Getting bombed isn't glamorous, or fun. Another glass of that stuff will make you throw up. That's before you pass out, if you're lucky."

Her eyes flickered. She laid her head down against the back of the spa. "I'd rather," she began, "kiss you . . . than pass out."

Nick entered the steamy waters again. He lifted Faith in his arms and carried her to a nearby lounge. She didn't protest, but flashed him a sexy smile. Setting her down carefully, he retrieved a towel and draped it over her body, rubbing away as much moisture as he could. Faith's eyes drooped closed and her head fell back. "I'm . . . sleepy, Nick."

"Hold on, honey." Nick lifted her up again, wrapping her arms about his neck for support. She snuggled her wet, delicious body into him. Nick groaned painfully.

Halfway up the stairs, Faith's eyes fluttered open. Looking seductive and smashed out of her mind. "Are . . . you . . . taking me . . . to bed?" she asked softly.

"Yeah," Nick responded.

She smiled. "Will you make love to me?"

"Yeah."

She closed her eyes and pressed her breasts into his chest as she snuggled closer.

Nick was thankful he'd reached her bedroom. Tossing back the covers, he laid her down. "But, not tonight, Irish," he whispered. "I want you to be conscious when I make love to you."

"Mmmmm." She melted in the comfort of the sheets, burrowing her head into the pillow. "Good night, Nicky," she murmured.

Nick glanced down at her wet bathing suit. He didn't dare remove it, but as he began backing out of the room, he noticed goosebumps rising up on her flesh. Nick cursed silently. He couldn't very well leave her in this state, although the alternative would keep him from sleep the rest of the night. Still, he had no choice.

He bent down and loosened the strap of her top, then lifted her body carefully, to undo the tie in the back. She didn't stir, but her soft moan nearly did him in. He peeled back her bikini top, revealing beautiful, full breasts in all their glorious nudity. Nick took a deep steadying breath, but rapidly sucked in that breath when Faith moved slightly, treating his fingers to one soft swell as her skin brushed by him.

Even in her sleep, Faith's body responded to him. Her nipples peaked, glimmering in the dimly filtered moonlight coming through the window. He took a moment to torture himself with the beautiful sight, before efficiently removing her suit bottom and covering her up to the chin with blankets. "Good night, Irish," he said quietly, pressing a soft kiss to her forehead.

Nick walked down the stairs, out into the yard, and

dove into the pool. The fresh, cold water cooled his heated body and helped to quell his desire for Faith.

He doubted he'd ever feel with another woman the sensations he felt with her, however much he fought them, however cold the water. Faith brought out emotions he thought himself incapable of ever feeling again.

And astoundingly, Nick found he wanted more than another fling with her, although lusting for her had taken up most of his time lately. But Nick was a realist. He'd always been honest with himself. He knew he wanted much more with Faith. He wanted all of her. And he wanted the woman he knew she was, deep down inside.

She'd run out on him once before. If he gave in to his feelings and trusted her, she might bolt again.

Nick wasn't willing to take that risk.

Faith woke up scratching her wrist. The skin under the bracelet tingled, but the area wasn't even red or swollen. That was strange.

Faith sat up in the bed to take a better look at her wrist. As soon as she did, her head pounded—a hard, steady knocking that only intensified when she moved. She stopped moving. To think she'd asked for this.

Well, she'd certainly gotten smashed out of her mind, just as she'd intended. The morning chill made her shiver—and made her realize that she'd been sleeping totally naked.

A little voice penetrated through her foggy head. *You never sleep naked.*

Her brain, fully alert now, conjured images of Nick Chandler, the spa, the wine, the flubbed seduction.

She rubbed her tingly wrist.

Her head throbbed.

Faith slowly lowered herself down, cushioning her head on a soft pillow as she closed her eyes. She could simply stay in bed for the next week so she wouldn't have to face Nick. Or she could bravely go downstairs now. Neither option held much appeal.

Faith hunkered under the covers. What had she been thinking last night? In her own defense, she hadn't been sure Nick would join her in the hot tub. She's drunk a little wine to bolster her courage, and as soon as she'd invited him to join her, she'd made a fool out of herself.

Nick had behaved like a gentleman. He'd stopped her drinking so she wouldn't get sick to her stomach. He'd carried her to bed when she'd nearly passed out. He'd . . . Faith gasped. "He took off my clothes!"

She frowned. "Then left me alone." She sat up, ignoring her hammering head and the annoying tingle in her braceleted wrist. Legal jumped on the bed and crawled over to her. He licked her hand. She stroked his belly. It had become a morning ritual. "Now what, Legal? If I only knew what Nick was thinking. On second thought, it's better if I don't know. But he—he wants me. And I didn't think I wanted him to—but last night, I guess I did. And now, I'm completely confused. I don't know who I am anymore, Legal Beagle."

The dog lifted sympathetic eyes to her. "You do understand, don't you." Faith lowered her voice as she continued to pet her confidant. "And now I don't know if I should thank Nick or be insulted he put me in my place. Literally." She laughed ruefully, then braced her head from the ache her laughter caused. "Ouch!"

Faith dressed slowly, slipping on a pair of denim shorts and an old tank top. She left her hair down, since she couldn't imagine putting one bobby pin in her head. Grudgingly, she looked in the mirror. "Since when is Nick Chandler noble?" she asked her reflection.

Five minutes later, after a dash of makeup to brighten her pale, sallow face, she slipped on her sandals and made her way downstairs to the kitchen. With luck, Nick would be working. She could have the kitchen to herself, postponing their inevitable encounter.

Today wasn't her lucky day because there he sat, with a cup of coffee, a plate of scrambled eggs and toast next to him. Unaware that she was watching him, he appeared deep in thought, staring at something on the table. She studied his strong profile for a moment and followed the direction of his gaze. His mother's unopened letter came into view.

"I'll get you a cup of coffee," he stated dryly.

Faith jumped. She didn't think he knew she was standing there. "I'll take the whole pot," she responded, once she recovered from her surprise.

Nick curved his lips up in a small smile as he slid a mug of steaming brew towards her. Faith sat down. "Do I die of humiliation now?"

"If that would make you feel better."

"Nothing could do that," she said flatly.

Nick gave her a serious look. "Did you get sick?"

"No. I suppose I should thank you. The details are hazy, but you were quite wonderful to me last night."

He shrugged and sipped his coffee. "That's me, Mr. Wonderful."

"Nick, I really do want to thank you. I was so out of line—"

"You're welcome, Faith. Now, forget it. But next time you throw yourself at me, make sure you can follow through, okay?" He winked, but no smile appeared. "I'm glad you didn't get sick."

Faith let drop his remark about following through. She looked him over and realized she cared more about Nick's mental state than her own embarrassment at the moment. His eyes held no sparkle and his unshaven face, covered in a two-day stubble, couldn't disguise a clearly withdrawn expression.

Nick ran his hands over his face, then massaged his temples. He continued to look at the ivory envelope which contained his mother's letter. Faith, unable to remain quiet, placed her hand on his arm. "Why don't you open it? I'll leave you alone—"

"No," he rushed out, taking her hand and squeezing it slightly. "I'll open it . . . if you'll stay."

For that one brief moment, this virile, handsome, confident man had looked like a desolate little boy who'd been abandoned by his mother. Faith's heart fluttered. She had to stay. She couldn't bear for him to be alone if opening the letter brought him more anguish. "I'll stay."

He nodded and then, in one swift move, ripped open the envelope and scanned the letter before Faith had taken another sip of coffee. She watched as he reread it, then folded the single sheet neatly and put it back into the envelope. He was silent for several minutes.

Faith was dying of curiosity, but she waited patiently. If he didn't want to explain, that would be okay. She was just glad he'd read what his mother had to say.

Nick's fingers absently stroked Faith's hand. "Your restraint is remarkable."

"You don't have to tell me anything."

"Are you sure you want to hear? This isn't your problem. I hate dragging you into this," he said, staring at the envelope.

Faith smiled softly and squeezed his hand. "I want to help."

Nick blew out a deep breath. His cold, unyielding gaze warmed when it met hers. "Well, she doesn't explain much in the letter. But she does want to meet with me again. She's coming to town on the tenth. She said Mrs. D offered the use of her house, if I agree."

"But Nick, that's in two days. It's a good thing you opened the letter. You've got to let her know."

He looked bewildered. "I don't have an answer right now. I never expected this."

Faith bit her lip, afraid to say the wrong thing. Of course, she believed he should see his mother, but Nick didn't need any pressure from anyone, much less her. He had the right to make this decision by himself. He'd earned that right when his mother left him so many years ago.

Nick turned to her. "I need to clear my head. And you could probably use some fresh air right about now. Would you take a drive with me?"

When Faith hesitated, Nick added with more than a hint of charm, "You know I could have ravished you last night."

Faith blushed, wanting to ask why he didn't. "I would never have known," she teased.

"Like hell, Irish." His eyes raked over Faith's body, bringing on a heady rush of sensation. "Are you coming with me or not?"

The teasing, playful, wicked Nick had returned. Faith felt joyous relief. She didn't like seeing him look so miserable. "Are you sure you want me?"

"Well, removing your clothes and walking away nearly killed me last night." His dark brows arched with masculine suggestion. "Trust me when I say . . . I want you."

Faith came out of her chair and stood over him, bracing her hands on her hips. "You like leading me on, don't you?"

Nick stood too, towering above her. "No more than you like leading me on. Is it a date?"

"It's a date. But no more talk about last night, because I'm beginning to feel human again."

Nick only laughed, not promising a thing.


They drove east through Malibu Canyon and, upon reaching the Ventura freeway, Nick turned left, heading north. Faith had the feeling this was more than a leisurely drive. Nick seemed to know exactly where he was heading. They were quiet, taking in the rural California scenery. The freeway wound through pastures and meadows, lush and green from recent rains, and rolling hills dotted with grazing cows and horses.

Nick kept silent, deep in thought about his mother's letter, Faith assumed. And Faith, too, needed the quiet to help ease the hangover which had only now begun to subside.

They traveled north for thirty minutes and some

time shortly after, Faith must have dozed, because when she looked out the window, they were off the highway. Faith sat up straighter in the seat, glancing at rows of bushy cornfields to her left and red ripe strawberry plants freckling the scenery to her right. The long straight road turned onto one newly paved, lined with towering eucalyptus trees.

Faith stole a glance at Nick, whose mood seemed lighter. A small smile brought the edges of his mouth upward. "Where are we, Nick?" she asked.

"Santa Paula."

She nodded when he didn't offer more, wondering why he had driven them here. A question formed on her lips, but she wasn't given the opportunity to voice it.

"Be patient, we're almost there." Nick winked playfully.

Faith noted large ranch style houses on either side of the road, many surrounded by low-lying white picket fences. It was picturesque, a cozy little valley all of its own.

Nick turned onto a winding road that led them up a steep hill. He parked the truck and took Faith's hand as they made their way to the top of the rise. Awed by the lovely view and what would be a beautiful house, still under construction, Faith turned to Nick. "Is this yours?" Faith didn't need an answer. She'd seen the trailer Nick had told her was his temporary home when they'd first pulled up. It was fifty yards to the right.

"Yeah," he responded, not taking his eyes off the view.

"It's lovely. How long have you been building it?"

Nick laughed. "Too long. Tony got me this great

deal on the land, before the rest of the developments around here were built. It took me a year to draw up the plans and another year to get the permits in order. Since then, I've been taking my time, between jobs, working on the darn thing."

"You want it to be perfect."

"Yeah, I do. I've never had a real home of my own. Come on, let me show you around."

From the outside the house looked very much like the real article, but once Nick took Faith inside, she saw the work that still needed to be done. Basically, Nick's home was a shell, with three large bedrooms, a den, a huge kitchen and a three-car garage.

"I still need fixtures and I haven't decided on the two fireplaces. Brick, stone, marble, tile?"

"Nick, that's the fun part. You'll make the right decisions. I love the layout." Faith strolled over to the living room window. "You made the best use of the sun. This room will always be bright and cheery, but during the hottest part of the day, you'll be in the shade."

Faith continued to stroll through the house, noting the detail he'd put into his work, something she had come to recognize since working with him on the room he was converting for Hope and Tony. "I love the archways and the vaulted ceilings. So airy." Faith twirled around, imagining each room complete, filled with decor that would define the house as well as the man who would live in it. "Are you going to stay and work on it when your work for Tony is done?"

Nick gave her a long look. He rubbed his jaw. "I haven't decided. I have two job prospects. One would take me out of town, the other is local. It depends on . . . certain things."

Faith nodded and continued to walk through the rooms. Nick followed her, wearing an amused smile. "What?" she asked finally, when she'd had enough of his smart-aleck grins.

"Nothing."

"Nothing? Then why are you looking at me like that?"

"I'm enjoying your enthusiasm."

"I like your house." Faith lifted her chin. "I've paid you a dozen compliments. You have yet to thank me."

"Thank you," he said with a smile that nearly charmed her socks off.

"That's better. I'd love to see the grounds."

Nick unlatched the back door and guided her outside. He kept his arm lightly around her waist. "Take a deep breath. The air is clean here."

Faith inhaled sharply. "And the view is dynamic." Their shoulders brushed. Faith leaned into him absently, enjoying the scene set before her eyes. The community was ensconced in hills and valleys, with dips and rises in the earth that lent beauty and contrast. Trees were everywhere.

"I know Tony loves the ocean. Most people do, but I'm more the mountain type. Give me an uncharted trail in the backwoods and a backpack, and I'm a happy camper. Pardon the joke."

Faith grinned. She'd never seen Nick so obviously content in his surroundings. He seemed less volatile and more at ease here. "I've never been camping."

"Somehow I figured that."

"Sounds . . . adventurous."

"It can be. Or it can be the most peaceful time in your life."

Faith often wondered how she'd fare as a camper, alone in the woods with nothing more than daily rations and a slumber bag. Her friends who went camping had called themselves hotel campers, taking along every modern convenience, including televisions with VCRs in their expensive motor homes. Somehow, she didn't think that was how Nick would rough it. "Do you ever get lonely?"

His lips curved up in a quick smile. "I never said I went alone."

"Oh." Faith turned away and began walking back into the house. She hadn't mistaken his meaning. She had no business feeling this way. She and Nick weren't involved. Nonetheless, the thought of Nick Chandler out at some remote spot in the woods with a female companion made her edgy. And now, unwittingly, she'd shown him how he affected her.

"Hey," he said, taking her arm once he caught up to her. "I was joking."

Faith put her head down. "Doesn't matter."

Nick took her shoulders, drawing her to him. She thought he was going to ask for an explanation, but he didn't. "Do you want to see where I'm going to build the stables?"

Relieved he hadn't pressed her, Faith's interest sparked. "You're going to have horses?"

"Someday. I have to settle down first. But it's always been a dream of mine."

Nick took her down a narrow path where the ground sloped into another level area. "I'll build the stables right here. There's a horse trail just up the road a bit, leads into the hills. Some people go up on mountain bikes. I've hiked halfway."

"How much of this land is yours?" There were no fences, since Nick had no neighbors at the moment.

"I own two and a half acres, but I'll landscape less than half. I like the land untouched. It's pure and honest."

Faith knew what Nick meant. He was a man who thrived on honesty. Complete honesty. "I hope to know you . . . when it's finished. I'd like to see this place the way you've envisioned it . . . just once," she said softly.

Nick made no comment. His eyes searched hers with unspoken meaning, roaming over her face, stopping to linger on her mouth. Faith shuddered inwardly, thinking he was about to kiss her again. Anticipating his lips touching hers, she held her breath. She wasn't entirely sure whether she felt relief or disappointment when the kiss didn't happen.

With the slightest nod of Nick's head, as if he had just made a major decision, he laced his fingers with hers. They hiked back up the incline and, instead of heading for the car, Nick steered her to his trailer.

Faith panicked. Sure, she'd thrown herself at him last night. But that wasn't *her.* That was the result of too much alcohol. And now, she had given Nick the wrong impression again. Poised and ready for his kiss, what else could he think?

"Maybe we should head back to Malibu," she said, pulling away from the direction of the trailer.

Nick tugged her back and led her up the steps of the trailer. "No way. I have needs, Faith. And they can't wait."

# EIGHT

"It's larger than it looks," Faith said, glancing at Nick candidly, and around the trailer.

Nick chuckled. "Thank you."

Faith never failed to amuse him. Her crestfallen look minutes ago had instantly changed to relief, when he'd explained his "need" was for lunch. Thinking about his mother and the unopened letter this morning had crushed his appetite. Now he was starving.

"There's a full bedroom, bath, the kitchen isn't cramped. It's home, until the house gets finished. Have a seat, I'll treat you to my culinary talents. But you only have two choices," Nick ventured, as he looked over the contents in his refrigerator. "Would you like a ham and cheese omelet or leftover pasta?"

"How old is the pasta?" Faith said, taking a seat in his small kitchen alcove.

Nick sniffed the carton of takeout from Antonia's Kitchen. "Oops, too old. It's been here since before the wedding." He dumped the pasta into the trash can. "Omelets it is."

Faith chuckled. "Sounds like a good idea. Can I help?"

"Why don't you mix up some lemonade, unless

you'd rather have a beer?" He slid her a sideways glance.

She cringed. "Ooooh! Don't mention alcohol. My head has finally cleared."

Nick cocked his head back, but refrained from laughing when Faith's eyes fixed on his. Setting out all the ingredients, he handed Faith a wooden spoon. "Lemonade then."

Nick made the omelets, while Faith set the table in his cozy kitchen area. Within five minutes, they both took their seats. "Do you like the paneling in this trailer?" Nick asked, while forking a bite into his mouth.

Faith plastered on a polite smile. "It's nice. Why do you ask?"

"I'm thinking of using the same paneling for the living room and den in the house. Practical and sturdy. I'd never have to paint."

Nick watched Faith swallow hard. "It's a little dark and—"

"And?" he asked, peering at her with his most innocent expression.

Faith sat up straight in her seat and blew a breath out of her rosy-hued lips. "And . . . well, outdated. It's okay for a trailer, Nick."

"Oh, I'll have to remember that," he said, nodding. "Then you probably think black lacquered kitchen cabinets would be too dark also."

Faith bit her lip. "No. If that's what you like. But I . . ."

"What?" Nick asked, taking in her solemn expression.

Faith shifted in her seat. She sipped her lemonade and shrugged. "Nothing."

"I like the Formica on the counters in here. I thought I'd find a butcher block pattern for the house."

"For your beautiful kitchen?" she shrieked.

Nick rubbed his jaw. "Yeah. What's wrong, Faith?"

Nick hid his amusement, watching Faith squirm. He continued, "Of course, I wouldn't choose a shade this dark. I think you're right. Dark can be oppressive. I'd go with a lighter Formica."

Faith's eyes nearly bugged out. She used both of her hands to draw the hair away from her face, then clasped her head in her hands. She sat way back on her seat. "Nick."

Nick took another bite, concentrating on his food. "Hmmm?"

"You can't be . . . serious?"

"You don't like butcher block?"

She closed her eyes momentarily and chose her words carefully. "You've obviously spent a great deal of time and money on this. The house will be magnificent. I mean it, Nick. It's got style, without being ostentatious. You haven't overlooked a single detail. Of course, I'm only an amateur. But I'd hate to see you . . . well . . ."

Nick gave her his full attention. "Well, what? Spit it out, Faith. I can see there's something you want to say."

Faith inhaled sharply, then blew out the breaths in slow spurts. "Ruin it, Nick."

"Ruin it?" he repeated softly. When he looked into her eyes, she nodded slowly. "I told you I didn't have a gift for finish work. I build houses," he said, noting the pride in his own voice. "And I do a damn good job, if I do say so myself."

Faith looked miserable. Nick almost felt guilty. "I'm sorry. It's just that, well—maybe you should look into hiring someone to help with the decorating."

"Hire someone—hmm. A stranger?" Nick mulled over the idea, shaking his head. "No. I don't think so."

"Why not?"

"For one, I couldn't afford a decorator's fees. And two, more importantly, I want this home to be my own creation. I've never had a home of my own. This is a first. I couldn't trust someone who doesn't know me, someone I don't know, to make my house a home."

Faith looked stricken. She glanced out the window to the house in the distance. "Oh, too bad. But Nick, please don't go with Formica or black lacquer or—"

Nick raised his eyebrows. "You could do it."

"Me?" Faith squeaked out. "Oh, no. Nick, I wasn't implying that I should do the job. I'm not a professional."

"I'd pay you. You'd be doing me a big favor."

"No." She shook her head adamantly.

Nick persisted. "What about the work you did on Hope and Tony's office? That room wouldn't have turned out so well without your help."

She kept shaking her head. "No."

"We can take one room at a time."

"I don't have time! Are you forgetting I'll be going back to work at the library on Monday? And I'm renovating my own condo."

"I'm in no rush. You could work weekends. I'll pay you for your services. You can apply the extra earnings to decorating your place," Nick said, setting down his fork.

Faith stopped shaking her head to stare at Nick. A sudden understanding dawned and she frowned. "You had this planned from the beginning, didn't you? Entice me with your beautiful home, then pretend to make really stupid decorating choices so I'd be appalled and come to your rescue."

Nick pursed his lips and sighed. From the green fire sparking in her eyes, he figured she wouldn't buy a denial. And besides, he was too honest to make one. "Okay, so I wouldn't put butcher block Formica on my counters, but I know I'd make mistakes. Costly mistakes. I'm really no good at decorating. You would be rescuing me in a sense."

Faith got up from her seat to pace the narrow trailer kitchen. "Nick, this is really unfair."

"Why, because the thought of having a whole home to decorate appeals to you?" He had a feeling she'd love nothing better than to decorate his home

"It's not what I do. I'm a . . . a librarian."

*Keep telling yourself that,* Nick mused. She was hiding from the truth, running away from the woman she wanted to be. He couldn't think of another soul he would rather work with, putting together the rooms of the house that would be his home.

He stood to face her. "Then, do this as a hobby. A money-making hobby. Come on, Faith. We can work out the details later, just say yes."

"When did this brilliant plan pop into your head?" she asked ruefully, in a voice that clearly wouldn't be mistaken as sweet.

Nick ignored her sarcasm and took her hands in his. "This morning, on our little hike. About the same time I decided to agree to meet with my mother."

Her tense face softened. "Oh, Nick."

"Yeah, I thought about it long and hard. I may be setting myself up, but I'm willing to give her another chance." Nick pulled Faith close, taking her arms and wrapping them around his waist.

"You won't be setting yourself up. She's making an effort. She wouldn't do that if she intended to hurt you. I'm sure of it."

"That's what I'm counting on, Faith. Your intuition is good when it comes to other people. So, will you take on my business proposition?"

Faith stared at him for a long moment. "Do I know you well enough to make those kinds of decisions?"

Nick grinned. "You know me better than you know yourself."

Faith stiffened in his arms, but he wouldn't allow her to pull away. "And I suppose you're an expert on women?"

A small laugh escaped his lips. "No, never claimed to be. Just you."

Faith said coyly, "Ah, I see. You think you know what I want."

Nick brushed the backs of his fingers across her soft cheeks. "Yeah, I know. It's the same thing I want, only you're afraid to admit it."

"Nick, don't." Faith stepped back, out of his arms. Nick let her go.

"I won't, not now. When you realize what you really want, you'll come to me, Irish." Nick could be patient. He just hoped Faith wouldn't take too long. He was dying a slow death from wanting her.


Nick peered into the home office, taking one last look at his handiwork and gave a satisfied grunt of approval. The carpet guys had finished late this morning, so he was now able to view the room the way Hope and Tony would see it in just a few days. Completed. Nick knew they would be pleased.

Faith hadn't been here when the new carpet was being installed. She left him a note on the kitchen counter early this morning, saying she would be out most of the day, but wished him luck with his mother. She said she hoped they could work out their differences, because both he and his mother deserved another chance.

Nick had folded the note neatly and taken it up to his bedroom. He placed it in the pocket of the shirt he was to wear today, wishing that Faith had stayed to give him her words of encouragement.

She had seemed to understand his reluctance to meet his mother, yet she hadn't pressured him in any way. Perhaps she instinctively understood that he needed to resolve the issue of his mother's abandonment of him before he could really trust any woman.

And Faith had to know by now that her running away had shaken him to the core on that long-ago night.

Yet he wanted her, more than he had ever wanted any woman.

Even if she remained the straitlaced, apprehensive little librarian with the heart of gold, he'd accept her, bun and all. He'd take her on any terms because . . . he loved her.

Wow. He did love her. Last year, for one beautiful night, she'd made him feel whole again. He thought it had been a fluke, but meeting her again, spending time with her had confirmed his beliefs. She *was* the one.

She made him trust in himself again and, in doing so, made him realize he could begin to trust others.

Faith.

The name suited her to perfection.

Although he might be setting himself up for a terrible fall, Faith was a risk worth taking.

And tonight, he'd tell her.

Nick showered, shaved, splashed a healthy dose of cologne on his face, then dressed. Donning a clean pair of jeans and a white buttondown shirt, he glanced at his reflection. "You have it bad, Nick Chandler," he said with a grin, then whistled all the way down the stairs, out the door and into his truck.

Only once on the road did his thoughts turn to his mother and the confrontation he was ready to meet head on. Drawing a deep breath, he knew for certain he could do this. Hell, he felt so damn good, he knew he just might forgive the woman for abandoning him. She must have had good reason. He'd wait to hear her out before making a final judgment.

Nick turned the corner and parked in front of Mrs. D's house. He stared at the house that had become his second home while growing up, mustered all of his courage and got out of the car.

Mrs. D was on the porch waiting for him. He took the robust woman in his arms and gave her a kiss on the cheek.

"Nicky, it is good that you have come."

Nick nodded. "Is she here?"

"Yes." Mrs. D took hold of his arm and squeezed gently. "I'm glad you made this decision. Your mother is nervous, but I know you must be too. Please, take time and listen. For your sake and hers. And remember, Nicky, I love you."

"Ah, Mrs. D. You know I feel the same. And thanks." Nick hugged her tightly. "You've been too good to me."

"You deserved it. Now," the sweet-natured woman said seriously, then took his hand, as if she were leading a young child to his first day of school, "it's time to go in."

Mrs. D opened the door and took Nick into the living room. As the door closed quietly from behind, Nick glanced at the people seated on the sofa. Two anxious faces lifted up to greet him. One, his mother's, was the same rosy-cheeked face, slightly weathered from age, but just as lovely as he remembered. She stared at him with quivering lips and tears welling in her eyes. The other belonged to an adolescent boy who looked very much like Nick, with dark brooding eyes and a shock of thick dark hair.

Nick swallowed the lump in his throat and approached them.


It was late. Nick turned the key in the lock. He hoped Faith was home, waiting on the other side of the door for him. He needed to see her, but the house was quiet and dark. He entered slowly, following the direction of a dim light coming from the living room. As his eyes adjusted, he made out a figure nestled in blankets, sleeping on the L-shaped couch. And another smaller figure sleeping with his floppy-eared head on her lap.

Nick chuckled and moved closer to both sleeping forms. He bent down and stroked the dog's head first, while keeping a watchful eye on the beautiful woman nestled cozily in the corner where both ends of the sofa met.

Legal raised his head lazily and yawned. "Shhhhh. Don't wake her."

Faith raised her head, looking confused. Her hair was down and adorably mussed. "Nick?"

"Hi."

When Faith sat up, Legal gave Nick a condemning look with his big toffee-colored eyes. The dog scooted further down on the couch, obviously annoyed by this disruption of his comfortable sleep. Faith rubbed her eyes, then smiled sweetly at Nick.

"Why are you sleeping here?" he asked.

Faith yawned and lifted her arms in a big stretch. "I wasn't sleeping. I was waiting up for you."

Nick's heart lurched. She'd waited for him. "Were you?"

Faith took hold of his hands and wiggled into a cross-legged position on the couch. Her sleepy gaze lifted to him. "Yeah, Chandler, I was. Don't keep me in suspense. I've been worried all day. How did it go?"

Nick leaned back, covering Faith's hand with his and placing it on his thigh. "It went well. I couldn't wait to come home to tell you about it." Even as Nick spoke those words, the rightness of them settled in. Faith was the one person he wanted to share this with, the one person he trusted to tell.

Faith closed her eyes momentarily. "I'm so glad for you, Nick."

"Faith, I have a brother." Even to Nick, his announcement sounded astonishing.

"Really?" She squeezed his hand. "Oh, Nick. A brother?"

"Yeah. Can you believe it? The little guy is eleven. Eddie—my brother's name is Eddie."

"And what about your mother?"

Nick sighed and rubbed his jaw. "Loretta explained everything. There were a lot of tears. I guess I was too young to understand back then. She said she had no choice. After she left, she had a complete mental collapse. My father had been very abusive to her. She knew she wouldn't survive if she didn't get away and she also knew she couldn't take me. Mentally, emotionally, she wasn't up to it.

"Back then, there weren't the safe houses and support systems that we have today. She entered a clinic and stayed there for many years. She wound up marrying a doctor who'd been helpful and supportive, about thirteen years ago. He practices in Cathedral City, near Palm Springs. Oh God, Faith, she apologized a hundred times. She said that she'd stayed in contact with Mrs. D throughout my childhood, so she knew I was doing okay."

"Nick, did she explain why she didn't come back for you after she got well?"

"She wanted to take me back, but she was afraid of facing my father. He'd made her life hell. She said she'd been in a fragile state, and only the love of her second husband and her son made her feel strong. Eddie had been asking her for years to meet his brother. She's ashamed it's taken her so long."

"Oh, Nick. She must have been suffering as much as you were."

Nick now realized how much his mother had been through. She had been as much a victim as he had. "I hated her for so long. She left me with that man."

"Nick, was he abusive to you as well?"

Nick flinched, remembering those days. "Not physically. By the time my mother left, my father was only interested in where his next bottle was coming from. Oh, he'd slap me around, but never with much force. He'd usually pass out before he could do much harm. It's over and done with, Faith. He died a few years ago."

Faith reached up to kiss him on his cheek, his chin, the corner of his mouth. The warmth of her lips felt like a healing balm. "I'm glad he didn't hurt you."

Nick enjoyed her pampering. It had been a long time since he'd let down his guard enough to allow someone to care for him, really care for him. He propped his head against the sofa cushion and stretched out his legs. "Keep that up, Faith, and I won't stop talking." He smiled at her.

Faith looked perplexed, deep in thought. She hesitated before asking, "What about Palm Springs? She didn't come to meet you that . . . that day."

The reminder of being abandoned, not once but twice, stung. And he'd almost forgotten that Faith had run out on him too. "She had a mild heart attack the day before we were to meet."

Faith gasped. "Oh no. That's why she didn't show up. I knew she had to have a good reason."

"Yeah, and she wrote to me when she was feeling better, but by then I'd taken a job up north. When the letter finally reached me six months later, I tore it up."

"So you never knew."

He shook his head. "I've always had bad timing."

Faith bit her lip. "Nick, do you think, I mean—I could understand if you can't—but do you think you'll be able to forgive her?"

Nick coaxed Faith's head down to rest on his chest. She stretched out beside him. His hand glided up and down her back. Stroking her gave him a sense of peace. "I think someday I'll be able to forgive her. It wasn't her fault. She made some bad choices, perhaps. I'm beginning to understand what she went through. She had it rough."

"Nick, that's very generous of you." Faith raised her head up to look into his eyes. "Do you plan to see them again?"

Nick's chest rumbled when he chuckled. "I'm invited to Eddie's twelfth birthday in January."

"Will you go?"

Nick lifted her chin to meet her lovely sympathetic green eyes. "Depends on you."

"Me?" Faith's voice rose slightly in surprise.

"I want you to meet them. In fact, there's so much I want to—"

Nick couldn't finish the sentence, because Faith brought her lips to his and kissed him soundly on the mouth. Nick, never one to miss an opportunity, cupped her head in his hand, drawing her closer. Her beautiful dark coppery tresses spilled onto his arm. With a groan, he deepened the kiss. It was potent and heady and long.

Abruptly, Faith pulled away, her chest heaving up and down. Nick wasn't in much better shape. In fact, his whole body responded to that kiss. And the most obvious effect was apparent directly below his waist.

"Nick, listen. I've come to a decision," she said seriously. "If the offer still stands, I would love to take on the job of decorating your home. I want it to be strictly business, though. I want to be treated like a professional. If there's something you don't like or agree with, you have the right to tell me, and I would do the same. I'll work evenings and weekends. You said you weren't in any rush," she finished persuasively.

"Okay." Nick was quick to agree. He didn't understand how that kiss prompted her into business mode, but he wasn't about to disagree with any arrangement that would keep her around.

They talked then, long into the night, sharing the stories of their lives, as if a door had suddenly opened between them. Their newfound intimacy quickly deepened into a sense of physical tenderness that brought them very close together in the tumble of blankets on the sofa. He held her as close as he dared, not wanting to rush her, but very definitely wanting her.

Then Faith said, "There's something else." She leaned across the sofa, stretching her body over the top cushion to the end table. She picked something up, then slowly put it in his hand. Nick glanced down at a small bottle of massage oil, then looked up to question her with his eyes. "I've been saving this . . . for when we were both ready. I want you to put this on me, slide your hands over my body and, oh yes, make me moan your name."

Nick's mouth dropped open. He stared at her. A wicked twinkle sparkled in her eyes. Nick blinked. She nodded.

"Well?" she asked, running her hands over his chest. She teased at the top button of his shirt, then quickly undid it.

Nick sat up and grabbed both of her hands. His heart pounded hard and fast. "Are you sure?"

Faith rose up on his legs and straddled his thighs. That was enough of a surprise, but then she lowered her lids, casting him a seductive look, and whispered, "Hurry, Nick. I ache all over."

She pressed herself closer. She wouldn't have to ask again. He twisted the cap off the bottle of oil. "Ah, finally, Irish, but there's no hurry. We have all night."

He began by rubbing the massage oil onto her soft shoulders.

# NINE

Moaning his name came easy. Nick kissed her again and again, dozens of times, until Faith became lost in a storm of passion. He removed her clothes with such finesse that Faith didn't know what was happening until the deed was done.

Pressing her down onto the sofa, he stood to remove his own clothes. Faith had seen him this way once before: aroused and magnificent, a mass of muscled chest and rigid torso, so masculine, so appealing. At that time, though, she had only known the surface of the man. He had been a tempting stranger.

Now, he was Nick. Her Nick. She whimpered and reached out for him. He smiled and bent on his knees before the couch. "No rush, honey. I want to touch every part of you first."

Nick took hold of the bottle of oil and tipped it over her. Cool drops fell, meeting with the heat of her own skin. She heard a low, anguished groan, which wasn't hers this time.

Nick leaned to kiss her lips just as his hand stroked her throat. From there, he moved lower to her chest, cupping her breasts, spreading the lightly scented vanilla oil over them. Faith responded instantly by arching her hips, biting her lip, trying to keep from crying out. Nick's eyes shone as he witnessed her uncontrollable pleasure. He gave her a satisfied smile.

His hand moved freely over her body, and each time he touched her, Faith squirmed, or murmured his name, or pressed herself closer. She flung her arms up over her head and surrendered to Nick's erotic assault.

He caressed her everywhere, cherishing her body. Faith felt warm shudders move over her in waves, making her skin sensitive to his slightest touch, his boldest touch.

"That's it, Faith. Let it go," he encouraged in a whisper. "I want all your passion."

Faith circled her arms about his neck and tugged his head down. His lips crushed hers in an almost brutal kiss. He slid his fingers smoothly down her torso, rubbing in the oil. Lower and lower he teased, until he reached her sensitive femininity. She uttered an agonized sound of want. He stroked her there, over and over. She moved with his rhythm now. Slow, steady, building faster, then faster again. Nick pressed a finger inside, never missing the cadence of the stroke.

Faith cried out. The pleasure was too intense. Her body was on fire, enveloped in sensual ecstasy. "Nick, Nick," she called out.

Nick quickly took her in another wild kiss, as her body shuddered convulsively. She tugged on his hair and kissed him back crazily. Between kisses, he watched her in wide-eyed wonder, and she was not at all ashamed. The look on his face told her not to be.

He stood and looked down at her. "We have to go upstairs, Faith. Now."

He lifted her limp body and carried her. She nuzzled herself in, wrapping both arms snugly about his neck. She kissed his throat, feeling the rough stubble of his slight beard. "Are you going to ravish me?"

"Yeah, good and proper," he said with a deep chuckle as he climbed the stairs.

Faith tingled, the slow, building fire beginning to rise again. She felt dangerously wicked. "Oh, Nick. You're good, but there's nothing proper about you."

He kissed the top of her head. "I know."

"It's an endearing quality."

He opened the door to his bedroom, giving it a kick. Faith toyed with a dark strand of hair teasing his neck. "What's my most endearing quality?" she whispered.

Nick tossed back the covers on the bed with a flick of the wrist. He glanced down at her, taking in her delicious nakedness. "You have many."

She smiled. "Such as?"

He lowered her, setting her head against his pillow. "Mmm," he said, his eyes drifting up to her expectant ones, "you know when to shut up."

"Nick!" Her protest went unanswered. Nick's mouth clamped down on hers and she could hear stifled laughter in his throat.

He kissed her deeply, passionately, all thought of playfulness now gone. Faith's heart hammered. The blood pulsed through her veins, hot and thick. Nick lay down beside her and touched her intimately, all over.

Faith pressed her palms on his rippled torso and ran her hands over him. He trembled under her ministrations. She lifted up to tease one erect nipple with her tongue. Nick murmured a soft oath and lowered her back down.

He took her hand and guided it down, until she

was stroking him, her palm sliding over the hot, silky skin of his manhood, gliding up and down. He encouraged her with soft, seductive words until she needed no further guidance. Nick's face showed his pleasure, and his response brought her to a heightened peak of arousal.

He moved his body over hers. With a nudge of his knee, he parted her legs and thrust, plunging into the velvety depths of her. They both cried out, a low anguished moan of satisfaction.

Nick made love to her in a slow cadence that began to build to a pinnacle of elevated desire. And then, when Faith thought she might die from the incredible sensations pulsing through her, Nick brought her expertly to climax.

Then Nick reached his release, repeating her name, over and over.

And with the final plunge, he brought his lips to hers for one last exquisite kiss. He remained with her for long moments, his breathing ragged. Then he rolled over to lie on his back, one arm around her shoulder. Faith snuggled in, resting her head on his chest, relishing his warmth.

When his breathing had calmed, Nick spoke softly in her ear, "That, was definitely worth the wait."

Nick was a fabulously sexy man, but surely even he had to admit the time they'd known each other hadn't been overly long. "Hmmm," she said with a smile, "two weeks is hardly a record."

"Two weeks? Honey, I've been celibate for over a year."

Faith paused. Could he mean what she thought he meant? She'd jump for joy if he hadn't been with another woman since she'd met him in Palm Springs. "You have?"

He shot her a solemn look. "A man doesn't usually admit that unless it's true."

Her heart warmed with that notion. "But why? I mean, I know I haven't, I didn't . . . you know. But you, Nick? I guess I'm surprised."

"I'm glad you didn't. And that makes two of us—it surprises the hell out of me too."

"Oh." Then a thought crossed her mind. "But you had protection."

Nick chuckled, low and deep. "Yeah, I thought I might get lucky this week."

Faith punched him in the ribs.

"Ow!" He took hold of her wrists and kissed the lower part of her palms. "Okay, okay. But I really did just make a quick stop at the drugstore today. I guess for once, my timing wasn't too bad."

Faith played with the dark hairs spiraling on his chest. "What's that supposed to mean?"

"All my life, I've had bad timing, Irish."

"Are you saying that because you were arrested?"

Nick blew out a slow breath. He hesitated. "Yeah, that too."

"Tell me, Nick. I want to know everything."

Nick stroked her hair, over and over. She didn't think he would answer, but then, as if he'd placed himself back in time, he began. "It didn't much matter what I did. I always seemed to get caught. Sometimes I think I did it on purpose, just to get my old man to sober up and come get me at the police station. I did stupid, adolescent stuff. Shoplifting from the dime store, that sort of thing. Sometimes when I was hungry, I'd steal from the supermarket."

"Nick, you had a rough childhood, but you turned out all right. It doesn't matter anymore."

"Thanks for saying that, but it does matter. Mostly, I hated disappointing the DiMartinos. They were always so good to me. That one night, when I was picked up for stealing a car, hurt them the most. They probably felt betrayed."

Faith lifted her head to gaze into his eyes. He was staring up at the ceiling. "So why did you do it?"

"That's the crazy part. I didn't. Tony did."

"Tony?" Faith's high-pitched question revealed her disbelief.

Nick laughed. "I've never told another soul. Don't you ever tell anyone about this, honey. Promise?"

"I promise," she said with a quick nod, like a schoolgirl begging to be told the best and juiciest secret in junior high.

"One Saturday night, we were all so bored, there was nothing going on, nothing to do. I said good-night to Tony and some other friends and started walking home. I'm almost home when, next thing I know, Tony comes by in this hot new Thunderbird. We were jazzed. Tony swore up and down he was going to return the car right back from where he'd hot-wired it as soon as we went on a little joy ride."

Faith rested her head back on Nick's chest and continued listening to his story. She imagined him as a young boy, bound for trouble, hurting in so many ways. "So why were you arrested? Did you both get caught?"

"Hell, no. Tony had a curfew and his old man was tough. So, he panicked when he realized he was going to be late getting home. I told him I'd drop him off at home, then return the car myself. It was risky, but I had more experience with that sort of stuff anyway. I didn't want Tony getting in over his head."

"You were a good friend, Nick."

"Yeah, too good. Of course, when I parked the car in the owner's driveway, his daughter was just coming home from a date. She started screaming, her dad came rushing out, and next thing I know, I'm in handcuffs, being hauled off to jail."

"Tony let you take the blame? That doesn't sound like the man I know."

"He wanted to confess. He pleaded with me. I wouldn't let him. I told him he'd lose my friendship forever. I was bluffing of course, but he didn't know it. Hell, he had a good life going, a family who was proud of him. He was making good grades in school. The last thing he needed was a criminal record."

"Oh, Nick." Faith kissed him, then gazed into his eyes. "That was an incredible sacrifice. I'm proud of you."

Nick's eyes searched hers. "You are?"

"Yes. That couldn't have been easy on you"

"I didn't care what my father thought of me, but Tony's parents meant a lot. You know, I think Tony's old man caught on. The sly devil would look at me sometimes like he could see right into my soul. Shortly afterward, he offered me a job at his restaurant. I worked there, and put myself through college. Tony claimed he never told him, but the old man knew—he knew."

Faith's heart lodged in her throat. Nick's admission and the trust he'd placed in her tonight made her feel that she occupied a special place in his life. She sighed.

Nick looked down at her. "You tired, Irish?"

"No. I'm not tired."

"That's good, because a year is an awfully long time." He nipped her earlobe lovingly. Warm shivers ran up her spine.

Faith slid her hand down his chest, teasing the area just below his navel. "So, what do you want to do about it?" she purred.

He took hold of her hand and placed it where she might ease his tension. "Ah, Faith, you are a wicked one."

"You love me and you know it, Nicky." Faith gasped inwardly. She'd meant it as a clever comeback, but it had come out wrong. Nick's body stilled and she feared she'd made a terrible blunder.

The quiet of the dark room surrounded her. When Nick spoke, his voice was deep, laden with emotion. "Yeah, I do, Faith. I love you with all my heart."

Nick lay sleeping beside her with his arm draped possessively around her waist. His breathing was slow and rhythmic. He was tired, as well he should be. He'd made love to her most of the night.

It was four o'clock in the morning. Faith couldn't sleep, she could barely breathe. Thinking of Nick and his admission of love had caught her off guard. *I love you with all my heart.* She should be floating on air, but instead, a black cloud of uncertainty threatened to rain on her happiness.

The Triple Charm bracelet, like a manacle, was squeezing at her wrist. The pressure, which threatened to cut off her circulation, was overwhelming; and yet, when she touched the thin rope of gold, nothing seemed different. It hung as loosely as it ever had, dangling from her wrist when she shook her arm. She felt the tight, persistent ache as certainly as if she were secured in a rusty shackle. Her heart pounded in dread. She feared she knew the truth.

Since the moment she put the Triple Charm on, she thought she had only imagined its odd behavior. The tingling, the burning, the gravity-defying position of the second charm—she understood all of it now. The bracelet was trying to caution her. Up until this point, unknowingly, Faith had ignored all the subtle signs.

Yet these signs were important, and she could no longer ignore them.

Faith loved Nick Chandler, body and soul. He had to be the one. Her heart pounded "yes," her mind screamed "yes," but the bracelet, with all its mystical powers, was most definitely saying "no."

Faith couldn't be sure. She'd only worn the Triple Charm for a short time. She might be misinterpreting its meaning.

Slowly, Faith got up from bed, being careful not to wake Nick. She threw on his plaid shirt, which she found lying over a chair, and went downstairs to the kitchen with Legal, the loyal beagle, at her heels.

Faith made a pot of coffee, pondering her dilemma. Confused by this turn of events, she moved about in a daze. She rested her head in her hands and leaned over the counter, staring at the coffee maker as each deliberate drip plopped into the hot brew. She was certain she loved Nick, and the feeling was nothing like the wan emotion she had felt for Peter. No, Peter hadn't touched her heart the way Nick had. She'd never love another man the way she loved Nick Chandler.

Faith drew in a long, shaky breath. The pungent

scent of the strong, hot coffee permeated the room. "Legal, what to do, sweet puppy?"

Legal barked and playfully twitched his brown and white tail. "Shhhh," she said, reaching down to scratch his ear. "I don't want Nick to know I'm down here. Oh, Legal, I don't want to hurt him. I love him so much."

Legal yawned and looked at her in anticipation of another scratch. Faith obliged. "I never thought I'd fall for him, and now it's too late. Our love could only end in heartache. You see, Legal, he's only man number two."

Faith sat down at the kitchen table. She poured the coffee in a mug and took a sip, scorching her mouth. She didn't mind; the pain took her mind off the insistent pressure around her wrist.

A thought popped into her mind. She bolted upright in the seat. "Unless," she said eagerly, "I'm overlooking something."

Legal's ears perked up. Faith was sure the dog was part human. He understood her in a way few people ever had—except for Nick, who knew her inside and out. "It's worth a try, isn't it, Legal Beagle?"

Legal answered her with a low-pitched wail. Faith took out a pad of paper and a pen from the junk drawer and wrote Nick a note. She placed it on the kitchen table, then headed for her room to pack. "There's only one person in this world who has the answers I need."


Initially, Nick thought he'd been dreaming. He woke slowly, in stages, and his well-sated body told him that last night had not been a dream. He *had* made love to Faith. Again and again, he had expressed with his body how much she meant to him. And she had responded in kind and her every action told him she loved him.

With eyes still closed, he breathed in a light, fresh scent of her citrus shampoo . . . mixed with the smell of vanilla oil. He smiled, remembering those scents from their night of love. But as he opened his eyes to the morning light filtering into the room, he found he was alone. Faith was gone from his bed. His heart jolted. A feeling of panic and a sense of déjà vu set in. He recalled waking up another morning, one year ago, to see that Faith had gone.

But then reason set in. Glancing at the clock, he realized she'd be out for her morning jog by now. Faith was dedicated; she never missed her run.

Nick had slept soundly. She had probably tiptoed from the room earlier, not wanting to disturb him.

He sighed heavily. Just once, he would like to wake up with Faith in his arms. *Correction,* he mused, *every time.*

The beagle jumped on the bed, lay down and hung his head on his outstretched paws. Wearing a sad expression, he looked up at Nick. "Where is our girl, Legal?"

The dog closed his eyes. Nick knew the feeling. She'd be back soon, he told himself. Then, when he heard a commotion downstairs, he grinned and jumped out of bed. He began dressing quickly. Just as he finished zipping his pants, he heard a knock. "Faith," he called from the other side of the door, "you don't have to knock." He burst open the door, ready to take her in his arms.

Tony stood in the doorway. Nick blinked his surprise. "Tony? You aren't due back until tomorrow night."

Tony eyed him for a moment, then smiled sardonically. "That's some welcome, friend."

Nick threw a shirt on, leaving it unbuttoned. He frowned. "Sorry. How was the honeymoon?"

"Incredible. But there was a hurricane warning yesterday. Hope got nervous, so we booked an earlier flight home. I left a message last night on the machine. Obviously, you didn't get it."

"Uh, no. I was . . . busy."

Tony grinned. "So I gathered." He peered over Nick's shoulder, into the bedroom. "Sleeping late isn't your style, Chandler. What's going on?"

"Nothing much." Nick lied. He wasn't the kiss-and-tell type of guy, even if Tony was his best friend.

Tony thrust his hand in his pocket and came up with a pair of lacy panties. "I snatched these off the living room floor before Hope saw them." There was a mischievous twinkle in his friend's eyes.

Nick scowled, glaring at the small bit of lace. Very late last night, he had gone downstairs to let Legal out and noticed, scattered over the floor, the clothing he and Faith had hastily shed. He had scooped up all of the items and deposited them in his room. Obviously, he had dropped one very important item. And watching Tony's fingers wrapped around Faith's panties brought a surge of possessiveness that astonished him. He grabbed the panties out of his friend's hands. "I'll see that they're returned."

Tony said firmly, "Look, I respect your right to privacy, but we're talking about Faith here, aren't we?"

Tony's tone of voice was irritating. His friend was

looking at him as if he'd taken advantage of a school-girl. "None of your business, DiMartino."

"Nick," Tony said in a softer voice, "she's my sister now."

"Well, what the hell did you expect? You and Hope set us up. Isn't this what you wanted?"

"Hey, you make it sound so contrived. Yeah, I knew you'd be working here and, by the way, the home office renovation is exceptional. Hope is down there now raving over it. I think she wants to nominate you for contractor of the year, she's so thrilled. But, you have to know that when you and I made the plans months ago, Hope had made plans with her sister, too. My bride just failed to tell me until a week before the wedding that Faith was relying on living here while her place was being redone. I didn't want to spoil Hope's surprise or disappoint Faith. She is okay, isn't she?"

"She's fine. Look, this isn't what it looks like."

"Listen, no further explanations are necessary. I trust my best friend and I know Faith can take care of herself." Tony shrugged. "I kind of enjoy looking out for her."

"Yeah, well," Nick said, taking in a breath that lifted his chest, "maybe I want that privilege for myself." After he made his pronouncement, he realized how much he meant it.

"You're serious?" Tony gave him a hopeful look. And Nick silently admonished himself for being irritated with Tony earlier.

Nick met his friend's eyes straight on. "I'm in love with her, Tony."

The friendly slap on the back came sharp and quick. Tony was all smiles. "Congratulations. She's a great girl."

Nick laughed, relieved. Tony had never judged him, but Nick had grown up thinking he wasn't good enough. Faith helped him see that he was. "Thanks." Nick folded his arms across his middle and leaned back against the doorjamb, shaking his head. "In fact, I'm crazy about her."

"Wow, all this in less than two weeks," Tony mumbled out loud.

"Well, not exactly. There's more to the story, but I'll let Faith explain, if she chooses to."

Tony gave him an inquisitive stare. "Sounds mysterious and now you've got my curiosity going."

"Well, hang on to it, because I'm not saying another word until Faith returns."

"Tony?" a feminine voice called out from the bottom of the stairs. "Is Nick up there?"

"He sure is, sweetheart," Tony called down to her. "Come up and say hello."

Once Hope reached the top of the stairs, she threw her arms out toward Nick. Hastily, he thrust the panties in his back pocket before she got a chance to see them.

"Where's Faith?" her sister asked, as if Nick should know.

Nick shrugged, feeling suddenly uneasy. "I thought she was out jogging. She should have been back by now."

"I see. Well, then," Hope said slowly, "this might explain where she is." She produced a small envelope from her dress pocket. "I found this note on the kitchen table when we arrived home. It's unopened. I assume you haven't seen it yet."

Nick glanced down at the envelope bearing his name, written in Faith's handwriting. The dread he had experienced finding Faith gone from his bed had abruptly returned. "No, not yet."

Hope put the envelope in his hand. "Maybe we should let you read this in private."

"No! Please . . . I'll just be a minute." Nick fought back his momentary panic. "I'm sure everything is all right."

His hand trembled when he ripped the envelope open and scanned the contents of the letter. He blew out a deep breath and folded the letter. "She went to visit her grandmother Betsy. She'll be back tomorrow night."

"Hmm. I wonder why she went there," Hope said. Tony simply shrugged.

"Think she would mind it if I—where does your grandmother live?"

"In Henderson."

Nick searched his mind, but came to a dead end. "Where's that?"

"It's a small town just outside of Las Vegas. They retired there several years ago."

Nevada? Nick hid his concern about Faith's sudden departure and agreed to meet the newlyweds for lunch in an hour. After they left his room, he sat on his bed, wondering what had been so important to Faith that she would travel five hours by car to see her grandmother today? Nick couldn't believe she'd gone at all. The only consolation was the note she had written him. He unfolded the letter and began reading again.

*Dear Nick,*
*   I'm sorry to leave so suddenly but I have to see my Grandmother Betsy today. I'll be back by tomorrow*

*night. Don't worry. Oh, and please give Legal the rest
of my sirloin steak. I promised it to him yesterday.*
    *I'll miss you,*
    *Faith*
*P.S. Last night was very special.*

Nick tucked the note into his pocket, patting it
with his hand. She hadn't run out on him. She was
coming back. But Nick wouldn't be here. Now that
Tony was home with his bride, Nick knew better than
to hang around. He'd leave word for Faith that he'd
be at his trailer in Santa Paula. She could contact
him there.

Nick's well-honed instincts told him something was
wrong. First, Faith's leaving, then her note, which
didn't explain why and lastly, Hope's odd silence. No
one was talking. It was too much to think about, on
top of everything else that had happened.

In the span of one day's time he had renewed a
relationship with his mother, learned he had a
younger brother and believed in a woman again,
enough to fall head over heels in love.

Nick packed his suitcase and strode down the
stairs. Faith had a good reason for leaving. She would
be back. He decided to grant her the most precious
thing she had given back to him.

His trust.

# TEN

"I'll get the tea, Gran. You don't have to get up." Faith watched the cheery-faced woman struggle to lift up from her seat, relying on a cane to support her arthritic limbs.

"Hush now, dear girl," her grandmother admonished in a thick Irish accent. "How often do I get the chance to entertain my granddaughter? The doctor says it's good for my circulation to keep moving. And Lord knows your grandfather does spoil me. The only time I'm fending for myself is when he's taking his afternoon nap. Aye, I love the man, but he does tend to dote."

Faith remained in her seat, giving her grandmother the independence she sought. She viewed the proud woman take down two antique cups and saucers from her polished mahogany china cabinet. The lovely pieces dated back to the early nineteen hundreds. Faith breathed a secret sigh of relief when her grandmother finally sat down, after serving the tea along with a plate of honey biscuits.

"I hear Hope's wedding went off well. I wish your grandfather and I could have been there, but as you see, I don't get around like I used to."

"Yes, the wedding was wonderful. I brought some

snapshots along to show you." She fumbled in her
purse to bring out a half dozen Polaroids for her
grandmother to view. Faith scooted her chair close
and held the pictures up to eager eyes.

"Ah, my Hope made a beautiful bride. Such a
handsome couple."

"Yes, they are very much in love. Tony is a wonderful man." Faith flipped through the pictures
slowly. Her grandmother focused on each one, taking
in each detail until a nod of her head told Faith to
move on.

When Faith came to a picture of herself, Grandmother Betsy took hold of the photo. "Ah, there you
are, the maid of honor. How lovely you are, dear girl.
And who's this handsome gentleman?"

Faith glanced again at the photo. Nick, looking
dashing in his tuxedo, held her elbow in a pose not
dissimilar to the bride and groom's. "That's Nick
Chandler. Tony's best man and his very best
friend."

"That man has a gleam in his eyes. Your grandfather had that same spark."

"Yes, and Gramps still does—when he's looking at
you."

"Oh, hush now, dear, you're going to make this
old girl blush."

Faith chuckled and gave her grandmother a loving peck on the cheek. "You two are a match made
in heaven."

"Aye, it's true. Fifty-five years of marriage." She
took Faith's arm and whispered conspiratorially,
"Your granddad still lights my fuse."

"Oh, Gran."

Her grandmother stared at Nick's image. "He's the reason you're here. That gleam in his eye is for you."

Stunned, Faith stammered, "How on earth . . . how did you know, Gran?" Was her grandmother blessed with second sight?

"Silly girl, that same gleam is in your eyes when you look at his picture."

Faith blushed. The heat prickled her skin. "I didn't realize it was so obvious." Or that her grandmother was so perceptive.

"Dear, when you say his name there's a lovely tone in your voice, there is. I'm not mistaking it."

"Well, Nick is very special. Oh, Gran, I don't know where to begin."

Faith confessed everything to her grandmother, leaving nothing out, starting with Peter and the broken engagement. When she was through, she sat quietly, waiting for her grandmother's advice.

"So now you're in love with this Nick?"

"Very much, Gran, but if I'm correct, he's my second love. Aren't there supposed to be three?"

"Aye, there's always been three. That's how the bracelet got its name. The Triple Charm never fails, dear girl."

Faith's stomach twisted. She couldn't touch her tea or the biscuit Gran had placed on her plate. "Not ever, Gran? Think back, please. Was there someone, anyone, you remember in our lineage that defied the curse?"

"Oh, Faith, please don't be thinking of it as a curse. It's a blessed gift."

"Please, Gran. Think."

Faith's grandmother closed her eyes and began rattling off relatives names. "There were your two older cousins, Kathryn and Megan. My own mother, Grace, your mother, bless her soul, Hope and . . . no. I'm sorry. The others as well held to the charm. Two heartbreaks, then man number three is the true love."

"Ohhh, I was afraid of that." Faith wanted to rid herself of the bracelet once and for all. She'd actually tried while on the drive up here to take it off, but the stubborn clasp wouldn't budge. Its grip, however, had slowly diminished, it seemed, the farther she drove away from Nick.

"What about Bill? I dated him for two months. Does he count?"

Her grandmother shook her head. "I'll be doubting that. Hearts have to break. Did he break your heart?"

Faith let out a wry chuckle. "No, not at all. He's glad to be leaving to spend more time with his son. We're good friends and I'm happy for him."

Her grandmother shook her head.

"I told you I met Nick the year before. We'd been together for one night. Maybe that counts?" Faith asked optimistically. She was grabbing at straws, fearful the whole haystack would soon descend on top of her.

Her grandmother's gaze roamed over her face, taking a quiet and studious survey. Regret and pain lodged in those old hazel eyes. "Number two is number two, I'm afraid. Did you love him at that time?"

"I was scared. I ran from him. I can't honestly say I loved him, or that he loved me when we first met. Oh, but Gran, I love him now. I can't bear the thought of losing him. He's been through a terrible time. His life hasn't been easy. If I break his heart, it could destroy him. I know mine will never heal. I'll never want another man ever again."

"Heartbreaks are never easy, dear child. And this one seems worse than most. You must do what is right." Her grandmother took her hand. "I know you'll not be agreeing now, but the Triple Charm is like a divine guardian. Trust in it and in your own heart." She patted her granddaughter's hand lovingly, casting her an encouraging smile.

"But Gran!"

"Listen to your heart, Faith. Do what is right."

Faith sagged her shoulders. "That's just it, Gran. I don't know what's right anymore."

"You will, trust me."

"One more thing," Faith began, "did anyone ever mention anything strange happening with the bracelet while they wore it?"

"Strange? I don't think I'm understanding your meaning."

"Weird things, like the bracelet getting hot, or a charm standing on end. Anything like that?"

"No. As far as I know, the bracelet is just like an ordinary gold bracelet. Except of course, for the magic of the charm itself."

"So nothing strange ever happened, not even when you wore it?"

"Not even when I wore it, dear girl. It was a cherished heirloom to wear with pride. That's all," her grandmother said in an apologetic tone.

"Oh, this is all so confusing. I don't have any more answers now than I did before."

"Stay here the night. Think on it. The answer will come to you."

Faith's mind muddled with her emotions and tears

pooled in her eyes. "Oh Gran, I'm so afraid of what that answer has to be."

Faith had to face Nick tonight. Tomorrow she would return to work at the library, and would return as well to her old way of life. No more excitement, no more freedom, no more Nick.

After calling from her grandmother's house, she discovered Hope and Tony had arrived home one day early. Nick waited for her in Santa Paula. She needed to speak with him. The sooner the better. Faith was a coward. She knew if she procrastinated, she'd never muster the courage to confront Nick.

She'd gone over and over the situation, until it pounded in her head with a dull steady ache. She had to break it off with him, now, before either one had a chance to get more involved.

She scoffed at that. How much more involved could they be? They loved each other. But Nick didn't know she loved him—and that would be her way out. Cruel, yes. Heartless, yes. But for Nick's sake, she'd play another role this time. She'd cast him off to save him from deeper heartache later.

Parking the car, she buoyed her resolve: she would be doing this for Nick. The lights were on in the trailer. Getting out of the car, she hoisted back her shoulders and sucked in a deep breath.

The trailer door opened. Nick stood on the steps of the porch, with one hand on the doorknob, grinning. "It's about time, Irish. I was getting worried."

The sight of him, after only one day apart, made her heart race. "Hello, Nick." She hesitated at the base of the porch. To climb those stairs meant close contact with Nick. He waited and when she didn't move, he took the steps necessary to enfold her in his arms.

The comfort, the tender care, the strength of his arms wrapping around her, made Faith want to cry. She closed her eyes, relishing the feel of him. His lips brushed over her throat, her chin, her cheeks, then took claim to her mouth. She kissed him back fervently. How could she not? He was all she'd ever want.

He clung to her, tucking her head into his chest. "I missed you."

Faith pulled back and straightened. "I'm tired, Nick. It's been a long drive."

He took her hand and led her into the trailer. "Of course you're tired. Did you drive straight through?"

Faith nodded and sat down on the plaid sofa, kicking off her shoes.

Nick kneeled down beside her, grabbed hold of her left foot, and began massaging. It felt like heaven. She didn't have the strength to pull away. "Yes. The traffic wasn't bad, but it took over five hours."

Nick nodded, taking her other foot and applying the same sweet pressure. "This feel good?"

Faith rested her head back against the sofa. "Mmmmm."

Nick's hands climbed further up her leg, stroking, rubbing, massaging. Waves of heat coursed through her body at his sensual touch. *Oh, I love you, Nick.*

"Why'd you go?" he asked in a casual tone, but Faith knew he struggled to keep his manner light.

She sat up, removing her foot from his hand. Nick straightened, searching her eyes. "I had to get away, Nick. To think."

"About us?"

"Yes, about us."

Nick took a seat next to her on the sofa. "Listen, Faith. This all has happened so fast, but the feelings we have for each other are real."

Faith took a deep breath. "That's just it, Nick. I, uh, I don't . . ."

He took her hand, stroking her fingers, one at a time. "You don't what, honey?"

Faith closed her eyes to the tears welling up. "I don't know." She yanked her hand from his and stood up. She braced herself on the kitchen counter and stared out the window.

Nick came up behind her. Strong hands encased her shoulders and slid down the length of her arms. The comfort those arms afforded made Faith shudder. In that moment she realized what she was giving up. The sharp blade in her heart twisted tighter. "I mean to say I don't lo—"

"You can't even say it, Faith," he whispered, a warm breath caressing her neck.

He was right. She couldn't bring herself to say the words. It would be the greatest lie of her life. Nick, gentle and sweet, was making this difficult. She had expected anger, resentment. She could have handled that by lashing out in return. This Nick, so understanding and loving, was too hard to turn away. "Oh, Nick."

"You love me. Don't deny it."

Hurting him now would be the most difficult things she ever had to do. But she knew that she would be saving him from further hurt. *Number two is number two.* Her grandmother's words rang in her ears.

"You love me the way I love you, Faith," he said again, louder, firmer. "We have a future together."

Faith whirled around. "No! We don't. We can't." Tears streamed down her cheeks. She sobbed. "I'm not the woman you want."

Nick stroked her cheeks, removing the moisture. "Maybe I was wrong about you. You're not the same woman I met last year, you're even better. More beautiful, if that's possible. And you're everything I want."

Faith silenced her sobs. "Oh, Nick. No. This will never work."

Nick lifted her hand and fingered the Triple Charm bracelet absently. "Why not?"

It seemed to throb around her wrist. "Don't touch that!" Faith froze, praying he wouldn't ask her why he shouldn't.

"Sorry. I didn't know it was that valuable."

The bracelet hadn't disturbed her since she made her decision to break off with Nick. She glared down at the piece of jewelry she had come to despise. "It isn't. Oh, Nick . . . I don't know how to say this. I can't see you again. Ever."

"Why, Faith?" he asked, calmly enough.

"Remember when you told me you've always had bad timing?"

Nick nodded, bringing his brows together. "So?"

Faith used the back of her hand to wipe away another tear. "So, you don't know how true that is." She took his face in her hands and reached up to kiss him softly on the mouth. "Nick, I'm sorry, very sorry," she whispered between another onslaught of sobs. Picking up her purse she walked out of the trailer toward her car. She felt the heat of Nick's gaze piercing her from behind.

\* \* \*

Nick watched Faith pull away in her car. He rubbed his jaw. Maybe Faith didn't know her own mind, or maybe she truly believed this sacrifice was for the best. But Nick knew she loved him.

And he wasn't giving up.

# ELEVEN

Nick Chandler hadn't walked into a library in years. As he begged his memory for the facts, it had come up with a gangly adolescent Nick at the age of sixteen. He recalled a certain blonde he'd had a crush on who worked as a librarian's aide. The girl was a senior in high school, a volunteer. He'd invented a history assignment as a reason to speak to her. That month, he'd spent more time around books in the quiet solitude of the library than he had at any other time in his life. But his plan had worked, and he wound up dating the luscious blonde for three months.

With luck, he'd be just as successful today. Only the stakes were much higher this time. A glance around the facility told Nick exactly where he could find Faith. She sat behind a large, cluttered desk, assisting a young student.

Nick ambled down the aisles, watching Faith from a distance. Her head was bent over a large research volume, and he noticed that her don't-you-touch-me bun had almost come undone. Several dark auburn strands curled around her face and others whirled along her sleek neck, making an enticing picture.

The collar of her long, conservative dress rested at the base of her throat.

Once the young student who was speaking to Faith had disappeared amid the rows of bookshelves, Nick wound his way around the back of the library to surprise her from behind.

"I need help finding a book on decorating," he said in a quiet tone.

Faith lifted her head up from her desk. "I'm sorry, I don't think we—" She turned to face him as recognition dawned. "Nick," she said breathily.

He stood in front of her now, drinking her in. In less than a week's time, she'd gotten more beautiful. How was it possible? And how could he have fallen so hard so fast? One thing he knew for certain, he wasn't going to make it easy for her to forget him. "Hello, Irish," he said in a low voice.

"What are you doing here?"

"Is there someplace we can talk?"

A combination of fear and resolve burdened her lovely expression. "No, that's not a good idea. We've already been through—"

"Relax, Faith. It's not what you think. I need your help on something. It's important, otherwise, I wouldn't be here."

Faith chewed her lower lip, then nodded. "Follow me."

She took him to a small table in the corner of the library, away from the steady stream of people. He pulled out her chair, before taking a seat next to her.

Body language told it all. Faith sat ramrod straight, stiff and unyielding. Nick leaned toward her.

"Okay," she said, blowing out a breath, "what's going on?"

Nick grinned. She tried her hardest to keep distance between them, but it was futile. Space alone wouldn't suffice. There was a bond that was undeniable. And of course, love. "You promised to help me with my house. I'm afraid I have to hold you to that promise."

She shook her head. "No. I couldn't possibly."

"Faith, I wouldn't ask if this wasn't important."

She kept shaking her head. Stark fear shone in her green eyes, making them look like dark emeralds. "Under the circumstances, Nick," she said with a heavy sigh, "you know I can't. I'd love to help you, but it wouldn't be wise."

"This time it really is business. Look, I have the contract all drawn up." He pulled the papers out of his back pocket and laid them on the table. Though crumpled, they were still legal and binding. "I'm giving you the most generous budget I can. Here's your salary, plus an added bonus if you finish in six weeks."

"Six weeks? That's almost impossible! No. It can't be done."

She said *almost*, Nick thought. That was a good sign. Yet, he'd save his trump card until last. It was sure to clinch the deal. "You're enterprising enough to get it done."

"But even if I agreed, which I don't, there's so much to do. Six weeks isn't much time for a house that large."

Nick let out a pent-up sigh. "I know. It's really not fair of me to ask."

"So why are you?" Faith raised her brows and gave him a speculative look.

Nick searched her eyes. He was taking unfair advantage, but it was for the best. He wanted Faith in his life. They belonged together. She would never refuse now. "I need to have the house ready in six weeks—otherwise, I don't get Eddie."

"Your brother?" Her voice squeaked in such a high pitch, three children perusing books nearby looked up and giggled.

"Yeah, my brother. My mother and I talked this week. Her husband wants to take her on a cruise for their anniversary. She thought it would be a good chance for Eddie and me to get acquainted. She's even willing to take him out of school. I'd have him for the entire week."

Faith was quiet a very long time. She stared straight ahead, a blank expression on her face.

Nick began softly, "I figure we wouldn't have to finish the whole house, just the rooms Eddie and I would need. Both bedrooms, the kitchen, the den. The rest could wait."

"I suppose the trailer is too small for both of you?"

Darn, he'd forgotten about that loose end. "I sold the trailer," he lied.

"What?" Faith turned to him, stunned.

"Well, I wasn't planning on sticking around. In fact, I was offered a job as construction foreman for a new resort going up in Vegas. I was just about to accept when I got the call from my mother. Now I think I'll hang around for a while."

Nick eyed her, his fingers swirling in a circular motion on the table. Most of what he'd said was true. He had been offered the job, but had no intention of taking it. He wanted to put down roots—with Faith by his side.

Faith stared at his hand, watching his fingers intently. "This is important to you?"

"You know it is."

"And I'm your only option?"

"Yeah."

"Would we have to work directly together?"

Nick winced. The words cut into him. She wanted to avoid him at all costs. And deny her feelings. "Some. I'll treat you like any other professional, Faith. You have my word."

Her beautiful green eyes closed momentarily, and Nick held his breath. When she opened them, she said resolutely, "It's important for you and Eddie to get to know each other. I'll do it. And I'll try my best to get the job finished on time. I'll only be able to give you a few nights per week, but my weekends are free."

Nick shoved the contract in front of her and quickly produced a pen. She signed the deal, then slid the papers back to him.

He wanted to slump in relief. Instead, he nodded calmly and thanked her. They made arrangements to meet Sunday to draw up plans.

Nick's strategy had worked.


Wearing her comfy pink-and-black polka dot pajamas and ready to devour a large bowl of feeling-sorry-for-myself chocolate ice cream, Faith sat herself down in front of the television set. She channel surfed until she found a documentary on the nation's rising crime rate. It was just depressing enough to suit her disposition at the moment.

A loud pounding at the door startled her. Ice cream dripped from her upturned bowl, landing melted drops of chocolate onto her sofa. "Faith, it's me, Hope."

Faith groaned, then set down her ice cream, shut off the television set and opened the door. She'd take care of the mess later.

"Oh, hi."

"Oh, hi," her sister mimicked. "Is that all you can say? I've been calling you for two days. Tony and I want to have you over for dinner. You haven't returned my messages. What's going on, Faith? We're worried about you."

Faith left the door open and sat back down on the couch, avoiding the chocolate smears. "I know, I'm sorry. I haven't felt up to company, that's all."

She heard the door close from behind. Her sister sat down next to her. "It's Nick, isn't it?"

Faith shrugged and let out a deep breath. "It's just *everything,*" she moaned.

"Oh, honey. Everything meaning?"

"My job, for one. It's just not as satisfying anymore. I used to love to go work at the library, surrounded by all that knowledge. The wisdom in those books . . . excited me. I know it sounds silly. And I guess I still feel the same way about the books, but the library isn't the same."

Hope tilted her head in question. "How so?"

"It's all so sterile now. We converted to a computer system last year. All the libraries will eventually go that way. The card catalogs are a thing of the past. No one really needs my help anymore. There's very little personal attention. Heck, some of those kids know more about how to access the information than I do."

"Okay, so your job doesn't thrill you. That can't be why you're so depressed."

"I'm not depressed."

"Right, and you aren't ignoring a huge smear of chocolate ice cream on your brand-spanking-new sofa, either." Hope fingered a pillow cushion. "By the way, I like the fabric."

"Oh, what's the use." Faith hoisted herself from the couch, wet the corner of a dish towel and dabbed at the stain. "There."

Hope grabbed the towel out of her hand, and scrubbed hard until the chocolate smudge disappeared. "Now, that's better."

Faith grimaced and sat down again. "Thank you."

Hope sat, too. "Getting back to your job—why not do something about it?"

"I'd love to start my own business."

"You would?" Surprised, Hope leaned forward, turning toward Faith. "Doing?"

"Home decorating. I've always loved the work, even if it was just redoing my own home. I had fun working on your home office and I think it turned out nicely."

"It's terrific. We love it." Hope's gaze traveled over the newly decorated living room as if seeing the transformation for the first time. "You've done wonders with the condo too. You have the touch, sister dear. And Tony and I could help you get started, maybe send some clients your way. We're in the real estate business, you know."

Faith smiled sadly. Tony and Faith would have a lot of contacts to send her way, if she ever dared to make her dream a reality. She'd gone so far in her daydreams as to pick out a name for her business. "You both are too good to me. It's just a dream of mine. But right now, my heart's not in it."

"I bet I know where your heart is. It belongs to Nick Chandler," Hope said smugly.

Faith knew her sister only meant well, but nothing could fix her problem. She'd just have to endure the pain of losing Nick by herself. Only, the hollowness in her heart kept getting larger each and every day.

"No, Hope. I'm afraid Nick's not the one—I only wish he was."

"I'm sure he feels the same way. Nick must miss you."

"Doubtful. I've worked with him for two weeks now, helping to get the house done before his little brother comes for a visit."

"And?"

Faith grabbed a square pillow cushion and hugged it to her chest. "And nothing. It's over between us. I think I've hurt him deeply. He only speaks to me about business. He's overly polite, the perfect gentleman and—" Faith closed her eyes momentarily, unable to reveal her suspicions to Hope.

"Faith, tell me. What about Nick?"

She bit her lower lip, shaking her head slowly. "I think he's seeing someone else."

"What makes you say that?"

"Well, the other night, after all of our work was finished, he couldn't wait to get rid of me. He got all dressed up. The man could have stopped traffic, Hope, he looked so gorgeous. Then on the way home, he picked up an expensive bottle of wine at the store, before dropping me off in front of the condo. He never even gave me a hint as to where he was going."

"Hmmm, I see. And that worries you? Tell me, what night was that?"

"Saturday night."

Hope gave her a serious look, one filled with sisterly concern. "You know, I probably should let you go on thinking what you're thinking, just to put some kick in your engine. Jealousy might do the trick, but it wouldn't be fair to Nick. He had dinner with us Saturday night."

"He did?" Faith's heart pounded with relief.

"Yes, and if you had bothered to answer your phone, you would have had an invitation too."

"Oh."

Faith and Hope sat quietly for a moment. She felt Hope's sympathetic gaze on her, but Faith looked straight ahead, staring at the blank television screen. "You want to know what kind of man I'm giving up? The day I left for Gran's house, I was so confused and disoriented and—"

"In love," Hope interjected. "And he's crazy about you, Faith."

"Mmmm. He's number two"

"So what?"

"Don't say that to me, Hope. You know as well as I do, there's no future for us. The charms, which I have come to despise, don't lie. I asked Gran." Faith stood and rubbed her throbbing head. "She said I must do what's right."

"But she didn't tell you to break it off with him, did she?"

"Well, no, not in so many words. She said I should do what I know is right in my heart."

"And your heart told you to dump the greatest guy you've ever met?"

"He's number two!"

"Listen, honey, charm or no charm, I was going to marry Tony DiMartino. It wouldn't have mattered what number he was. I knew it here," she said with deep emotion, putting a fist to her heart. "Faith, listen to your heart. That's the greatest magic of all."

"You really think so?"

Hope stood and wrapped her arms around Faith, capturing her in a giant bear hug. "I know so. Take the chance, honey. Nick's worth it."

Faith blinked rapidly, in succession. "He is, isn't he?"


Faith fluffed her long hair, giving it a final touch, before dabbing cologne onto her throat, her wrists, her ankles. She stepped away from the mirror and smiled at her reflection. The emerald green dress had served its purpose in the past. This time, Faith not only planned on seducing her love, she planned on securing her future.

The candlelit scene was set. A romantic arrangement of lilies and roses centered the dining table, which was adorned with an antique Irish lace tablecloth. Champagne chilled over ice. Faith promised herself only one glass tonight. She needed to keep her wits about her. And she also wished the charm bracelet would cease its intermittent burning. It was as if her wrist were having hot flashes.

When she heard the sharp knock at the door, Faith composed her jittery nerves. She had gotten Nick over here under false pretenses. She'd told him her washing machine was on the blink, and she couldn't work with him on Saturday because she had to let the repairman in. When Nick hadn't rushed to her rescue, she'd added that she hoped they wouldn't send the same repairman as last time because the man flirted shamelessly. That had Nick offering to stop by tonight to see if he could help.

When she opened the door, Nick took one long look at her, then said, "You're not having washing machine trouble, are you, Irish?"

Faith stepped back, inviting him in. "Well, my delicate settings do need adjusting."

Nick scorched her with a look. "And I'm the man for the job?"

Faith took hold of his arm, leading him into the dining room. With a tiny shove, Nick fell into the chair. Faith sat on his lap. "You're the *only* man for the job."

His jeans were bedraggled, his shirt had seen better days, his hair was in desperate need of a cut, but Faith had never seen him look so impossibly handsome, staring up at her with a hint of hesitation in his eyes.

Nick spoke sternly. "What's this all about, Faith? Pardon the pun, but you've put me through the wringer lately. And I can't tell when your hot cycle is going to turn cold."

"I love you, Nick."

There, she'd said it. Nick's eyes flickered, softened. She had his full attention now. "I want to tell you all about the Triple Charm and all that it means, but I'm taking a risk here, although I'm willing to do just about anything for . . . us. Do you still love me?"

"Is this another trick question?"

"Nick, please."

"With all my heart, Faith. I always will."

Faith closed her eyes briefly, then began her story. Ten minutes later, and winded from her explanation, Faith let out a heavy sigh. The burden had been lifted and she felt better than she had in weeks. "So you see, even though you're number two, I'm willing to risk it all. I think this time the charm is wrong. You are all the man I want, Nick Chandler. You are my heart, my soul, my love. Forever."

Faith scooted closer and wrapped her arms around his neck. He gazed adoringly into her eyes. "So you're willing to ignore the legend for me. Number two?"

"They try harder," Faith teased and wiggled her bottom into him. Nick groaned and shifted under her. He was already hard enough.

"You believed in this Triple Charm all of your life?"

Faith gave him a wide smile. "I believe in us more."

Nick grinned. "You're a hell of a woman, Faith Heather McAllister."

"So will you marry me?"

Nick chuckled. "I was planning to." He lifted her gently from his lap and dug into his pocket. He came up with a heart-shaped diamond ring. Facing her now, he took hold of her hand. "I wasn't letting you go, no matter what." He placed the ring on her finger. It sparkled, a bright beacon of love and hope and trust all rolled up into one. "I love you, Irish. We'll have a long, wonderful life together. Do you believe that?"

Faith hugged the ring to her chest, elated. "I do, Nick. With all of my heart."

Nick took her in his arms and claimed her mouth in a slow, taunting, deliberate kiss that made every nerve in her body tingle. When their lips finally

parted, Faith murmured, "I don't care what this ri-
diculous charm bracelet means, we belong together."

With a quick flick of the wrist, Faith shook off the
burning sensation. But as she glanced down, she
froze. "This can't be," she whispered in stunned surprise.

Nick grabbed her wrist and lifted. They both studied the bracelet. Faith twisted her arm back and
forth. "Nick, look, the third charm is gone! It's
gone!" Faith blinked, then blinked again, but the
charm didn't reappear. "Oh, my! I can't believe the
charm isn't there.' "'

Nick moved her wrist into different angles. "Sure
appears to be gone. When was the last time you took
a really good look at your bracelet?"

Faith didn't have to summon any recollection. She
knew the answer immediately. "That day I walked out
of your trailer, Nick." *And almost out of your life,* she
didn't say.

"So you don't know if it could have fallen off?"

"It didn't fall off. I would have known. I can't explain it. The charm just vanished, tonight. It just vanished." Faith shivered and stepped back into Nick's
arms. "What do you think it all means, sweetheart?"

Nick tightened his hold on her. A cooling sensation, like blue ice, graced her wrist just under the
second charm. Like a balm, it soothed her skin and
made her tingle. As strange as it seemed, the bracelet
settled on her wrist and Faith knew a sense of peace.

"I think my timing isn't so bad for a change. Not
bad at all."

# EPILOGUE

Nick watched his two girls sleep. Today was their first day home from the hospital. It had been an ordeal. Nick was a nervous father-to-be, but Faith made it through labor and delivery with flying colors.

The tiny redheaded bundle in Faith's arms cooed, before falling back into oblivion. Faith opened her eyes to him. A beautiful mother's smile graced her face. "Hello, new daddy."

"Wow. I'm a father, Faith. I still can't believe it."

Faith fingered their daughter's tiny hand. "Yes, and I'm a mother."

Nick chuckled. "It seems this little one has changed everyone's status. Eddie is an uncle. My new brother thinks that's pretty cool."

"Yes, and your mother, Nick—she's ecstatic about the baby. I'm glad you invited them to spend a few days with us next week. I want baby Heather to know all of her family."

"Heather is one lucky lass," Nick added, imitating Grandmother Betsy's rich Irish accent.

"Yes, because she has a father like you." A teeny squawk came out of his newborn daughter's mouth. "Oops, I think she's waking up. Time to eat"

Nick leaned against the closet with arms folded,

watching his daughter at her mother's breast. The little one made gurgling sounds as Faith looked on with adoring eyes. He had never witnessed a more beautiful sight.

"She's so sweet, Nick. I want to spend all my time with her."

"I'd like that too. But don't you have clients scheduled for next month?"

"I'm just renovating a game room. I could do it with my eyes closed."

That much Nick knew was true. Faith's home decorating business had really taken off. "Are you going to close down Designs By Faith?"

"I think so, for a few months. Then we'll see how little Heather does. She may want to accompany her mom to work sometimes. Then, when she's older, who knows, she may want to take over the business."

"Please, I can't stand the thought of her growing up. Dating?" Nick shuddered. "Let me enjoy her as a baby for now."

Faith laughed, nearly shaking the baby off. "Nick, I'd like to show her the charm bracelet. Will you get it down for me?"

Nick absently put his hand into the front pocket of his trousers. Fingering the charm he'd found between the cushions on the sofa in his old trailer, he smiled. This charm had become his lucky charm. He kept it with him at all times, a constant reminder of the treasure he had found in Faith.

Never one to tempt fate, Nick hadn't told Faith he'd found the third charm. The antique bracelet she'd been so superstitious about was nothing more than an old family heirloom severely in need of repair. The charms had become dull, devoid of any brilliance, and certainly lacking any mystical powers. But why trouble Faith with the news? She'd accepted the fact that, at least in her case, the second time was the charm.

Nick located the long metal safety box at the top shelf of their bedroom closet. He sorted through legal papers and documents, until he found the gray velvet jewel case. Handing it to Faith, he brushed a kiss on her forehead, then one on his daughter's. Two adorable little eyes stared up at him. "Tony doesn't know what's in store for him. Little Mary won't arrive until next spring."

"I know, it's ironic. Our daughter will be a few months older than theirs. Which means our little Heather gets to wear the Triple Charm first."

Nick cringed at the thought. He didn't want to think of his precious daughter going through any heartache at all. Much less because of a piece of jewelry that held no real magic at all. "I hate the thought of it."

"Nick, the bracelet did bring us together."

"Uh-huh." Nick wouldn't argue the point.

Faith gently set the baby down on the bed. Nick adjusted Faith's pillow so she could sit up more comfortably. She opened the box slowly. "Oh, it's still so shin—" Faith stopped midway, and glanced up at Nick; a look of utter amazement crossed her features. "Uh, you haven't done anything to the bracelet have you, sweetheart?"

Puzzled, Nick shook his head. "No. I was glad when you took the darn thing off the minute we were married. I haven't seen it since."

Faith bit her lip. "Then what do you suppose this means?" Faith swiveled the jewel case in his direction.

Looking lustrous and new, three bright, polished clover leaf charms adorned the thin band of gold.

Nick sucked in a breath and his hand went directly for the charm he kept in his pocket. He felt the ridged edges of the tarnished clover leaf and knew he was not mistaken. It was the same gold clover he'd found in his trailer—the one he'd kept secret from Faith for nearly two years. He stared at the bracelet.

"Well, I'll be damned. The third charm is back." He sat down carefully on his side of the bed and wrapped an arm around his wife. With the other hand, he fingered each gold clover charm, half expecting one to scorch his skin. When none did, he grinned. "Looks like it may hold some magic after all."

Faith smiled. "Good wife that I am, I won't say I told you so."

Nick chuckled, low and deep near her ear. "You know, you have charms of your own, Irish." He nuzzled her throat, then planted a soft kiss on her lips. With a snap, he closed the jewel case. "As far as mystical powers go, well, look what our own brand of special magic created."

At that, Heather Betsy Chandler . . . hiccupped.

# ABOUT THE AUTHOR

Charlene Summers resides in southern California with her husband Don, children Jason and Nikki, and her furry feline Snickers. She has a love for all things romantic, including warm sunny days, great coffee, and to-die-for chocolate. When she's not writing for Precious Gems, her favorite pastime is reading books from her growing list of favorite authors.